Kelly set her shoul... Paisley had halted, or... a dramatic pose in the sexy green dress. The blond guy took one look and stopped dead in his tracks.

"How do, ma'am," he said. "Let me introduce myself. Gerard Manfred Offenbacher at your service."

"You know, Gerard, I've never been to Texas before, but you're exactly what I imagined a genuine western cowboy to be," Paisley purred.

"And you seem like a lively little filly yourself. What did you say your name was?"

Paisley hesitated, glancing at Kelly, who gave her a stern look.

"Why, I'm Kelly Blake," Paisley said coolly.

Kelly Blake
TEEN MODEL

One day she's an A student at Franklyn High with a major crush on the boy next door. Then she's discovered by the head of the prestigious FLASH! modelling agency. Almost overnight Kelly becomes the hottest new face in the modelling world!

Each of the KELLY BLAKE titles features the ongoing characters and events in Kelly's life. While romance is part of that life, these books are more than romances; they deal with the experiences, conflicts, crises and behind-the-scenes details of modelling.

Ask your bookseller for the titles you have missed:

1. DISCOVERED!
2. RISING STAR
3. HARD TO GET
4. HEADLINERS
5. DOUBLE TROUBLE

Coming soon:
6. PARIS NIGHTS

• • • • • • • • • 5 • • • • • • • • •
KELLY BLAKE
TEEN MODEL
• •

Double Trouble

Yvonne Greene

BANTAM BOOKS
TORONTO • NEW YORK • LONDON • SYDNEY • AUCKLAND

With special thanks to
Abby Daniels, whose help
was invaluable.

RL 6, IL age 12 and up

DOUBLE TROUBLE
A Bantam Book/August 1987

*Setting of back-cover photo of Kelly Blake in the soda shoppe
courtesy of Antique Supermarket.*

ISBN 0-553-26154-1

Published simultaneously in the United States and Canada

*Bantam Books are published by Bantam Books, Inc. Its
trademark, consisting of the words "Bantam Books" and
the portrayal of a rooster, is Registered in U.S. Patent and
Trademark Office and in other countries. Marca Regis-
trada. Bantam Books, Inc., 666 Fifth Avenue, New York,
New York 10103.*

Printed and bound in Great Britain by
Cox & Wyman Ltd., Reading

Double Trouble

One

"Here's to Kelly Blake, and to her new, exclusive contract with the House of Noireau!" Lisa Daly drained her soda glass while everyone applauded.

Kelly, her blue-green eyes sparkling, held up her hand in protest. "Wait a minute, you guys, don't start celebrating yet. I may not get the contract. After all, lots of models will be in Houston trying to win this contest. As far as I'm concerned, I'm only going to Texas for a modeling assignment."

Jennifer Lee's dark eyes shone with pride for her best friend. It had been her idea to get Kelly's friends together at Campy's, a popular coffee shop, for an after-dinner celebration of Kelly's latest assignment. "You, not win? I predict that the Noireau people will fall all over themselves when they see you in action. If you don't win the contest, then—then they don't know a good model when they see one."

"I'll drink to that!" their friend Sue Levine cried. She and Rochelle Sherman clinked their glasses together.

"Thanks, but really, I know there's going to be stiff competition." Kelly smoothed her wavy brown hair. "Don't count on it, okay?"

"But you fit the bill," Jennifer argued. "You said the Noireau people want a new model on the way up, someone who hasn't been overexposed. You'd be perfect. You can represent their entire line—clothes, makeup, jewelry, perfume—"

"Jennifer, hold on," Kelly protested, laughing. "They might want a more European look."

"You can be any type you want to be," Jennifer said stubbornly.

"I don't know about that," Kelly said with a smile. At only sixteen, she had been exposed to a wide variety of assignments in the short time since she'd begun modeling, but she knew she still had a lot to learn about the business. "Hey, I'm starving. Who wants more fries?"

"None for me." Lisa patted her stomach. "I don't have your invisible waistline. I'm counting calories."

"Not again," Rochelle groaned. "Every time you go on a diet, I'm the one who suffers. You never want to go anywhere or do anything, because you're afraid it'll involve eating."

"That's not true," Lisa protested as Kelly

signaled the waitress. "I came along tonight, didn't I?"

"You had to come tonight. You couldn't miss our farewell party for Kelly. Imagine, Kelly going to Houston and missing four days of school."

"I can't believe your parents are letting you go," Sue said.

Kelly took a sip of cola. "They had to this time. They finally realized I had to accept out-of-town assignments or I might as well give up modeling, and they don't want me to do that. Besides, my first location job went really well."

Jennifer, who knew that Kelly's recent location shoot at a Long Island mansion had been a combination of disasters and triumphs, pretended to choke on her soda.

"The one with Mickey Pines, the movie star— how could we ever forget," Lisa sighed. "I'm going to save my copy of that *Couture* forever when it comes out. I still can't believe you actually kissed him!"

Kelly grinned, remembering her short-lived, far-from-perfect romance with the difficult young star. "Well, I guess we've talked my career to death," she said as everyone picked at the remains of their food. "What else is new?"

"Nothing much," Lisa answered. "Face it, except for you, we all lead dull lives."

"Sometimes I get so bored I could scream," Rochelle agreed, stifling a huge yawn.

Ignoring her, Jennifer laid a hand on Kelly's arm. "I hope you get a chance to call me from Houston. I'd call you, but my folks are all steamed up about our phone bill again. If I called

Texas, forget it—they'd pull my phone right out of the wall."

"That's okay, Jen. Maybe I can call. It depends on how many personal calls the client allows us to make. I'll have to call home, too. But I can always write."

"Yeah, but by the time your letters got here you'd probably be home already."

Kelly pushed her straw around in her drink, trying to smile. "I'll really miss talking to you every day."

"Don't be dumb. You're not going to miss me. You'll be so busy you won't have time to be lonely."

Kelly shot her a grateful look. Jennifer was the only one who knew how nervous she was about this trip. She had never been away from home on her own for very long before, and while she couldn't wait to see Houston, she had qualms about going. What if she got homesick? Just thinking about the trip gave her butterflies in her stomach.

"It's almost eight o'clock," Lisa remarked. "Whatever happened to Eric? I thought he was joining this celebration. He didn't have another date, did he?"

"Hey, forget Eric," Rochelle teased. "In Houston Kelly will meet the man of her dreams. I can see it already: Kelly in a slinky long gown, him in a dashing tuxedo and a cowboy hat. Their eyes meet across a crowded room and electric sparks fill the air. He walks toward her, his boots clunking across the dance floor. He sweeps off his hat and that's it. She falls madly in love."

Rochelle sighed dramatically. "And it doesn't hurt that he's a millionaire and he flies all your friends out to Texas to visit you, Kelly," she added.

"You guys are too much." Kelly smiled but glanced at her watch with some concern. Where *was* Eric, anyway? Had he forgotten about their date? It wouldn't be the first time. Sometimes he got so wrapped up with his car, track, or his ten-speed that he completely forgot about her!

She turned back to her friends. "Look, Rochelle, if this assignment is like any other, I'll be so busy that I won't even get to know the other models, much less meet your cowboy hero. Believe me, this will be a lot of hard work."

Rochelle sighed. "Yeah, and while you're suffering away in Houston the rest of us will get to lead our usual dreary lives. Just once I wish something exciting would happen here. What fun do we ever have?"

"Let's face it," Sue agreed, "Franklyn, New Jersey, is not one of the hot spots of the Western Hemisphere."

"It's the pits."

"You can say that again."

Rochelle lifted her glass for another toast. "Here's to the dullest town east of the Mississippi. The guys in this town—forget it! They'd rather get together to talk football than even dream of taking a real, live girl out to a movie."

"Or dancing, or anywhere else," Lisa agreed. "The boys in this town are a complete, total waste. How did we get stuck in a school with such a bunch of losers, anyway?"

"You can't blame it all on them," Jennifer said logically. "After all, we could make some effort, too."

Rochelle scowled. "Oh, yeah, like what? We try plenty hard to get them to pay attention to us. What else can we do?"

"I don't know . . . there must be something. Maybe we could come up with an event of our own, make our own excitement."

Lisa was skeptical. "Fat chance, Jennifer. Like what, for instance? *Your* idea of excitement is programming some bizarre calculations into your computer."

Jennifer took her ribbing in stride. "Come on, that's negative thinking. If we were really clever, we could get the guys interested in our hobbies. Even computers."

"Don't listen to Lisa, Jen," Kelly said loyally. "But maybe we *should* plan something that will get everyone involved."

"Like what? And don't say a carnival," Rochelle warned. "I had enough carnivals and fairs in elementary school to last a lifetime. The very idea makes me sick."

"No, not a carnival, nothing wimpy like that. I don't know, maybe something to do with sports . . ."

"I stink at outdoor sports," Lisa wailed.

"Well, okay, then, let's see . . . Hey, I know, how about a skating party?" Kelly asked.

"Oh, great. We'll flood the supermarket parking lot and pray for a cold spell to freeze it over. Have you lost your mind?"

"Not outdoors, Rochelle. An indoor party, at the skating rink."

"The skating rink! I haven't been there since I was twelve," Rochelle said. "Remember, every weekend one of our mothers would drive us there. I thought I was going to be an Olympic skating star."

"Your first major disappointment," Lisa cracked. "You could barely stand up."

"Seriously," Jennifer said, "maybe that's not such a bad idea."

"Are you kidding? That's for kids. The rink will be full of ten-year-olds."

"Not necessarily." Kelly leaned forward eagerly. "If we had enough people interested, we might be able to rent the place ourselves for one night."

"At night—a night skating party." Rochelle began to look interested. "That's different. You mean we'd have the place completely to ourselves, high-school kids only?"

"With a light show, like they had at the prom last year?" Sue asked.

"Or a live band?" Rochelle was getting excited.

"Why not?" Kelly said.

Jennifer frowned. "Wait a minute, Kelly. Is the rink even open at night? I have no idea what their hours are anymore."

"Look, if everyone's interested, why don't we find out right now. I'll call them and see if this whole thing is possible."

"No, you sit. You're the guest of honor," Rochelle insisted. "Besides, after all the money I've spent in that place, I figure they owe me a favor."

While Rochelle was gone they continued to discuss the idea. Lisa held her breath and measured her waist with her hands. "If I don't lose five pounds fast, I'm not going! I'll look awful in a skating outfit."

Kelly's eyes lit up. A skating outfit! *Let's see,* she thought, *I'll wear tights, a big sweater, no, maybe a long-sleeved leotard with a short skirt.* She could imagine Eric's face when he saw her, the glow in his blue eyes . . .

Rochelle returned from the phone booth. "Well, the man at the rink, Mr. Corelli, loved the idea. He said he's been trying to think of a way to get more older kids to come, so he said if we can guarantee a decent crowd that night, we can have the whole rink to ourselves, for free! I mean, we'll have to pay the usual admission and skate rentals, but we won't have to pay any rental fee. It'll be high-school kids only, and we can have a light show or anything we want, as long as we arrange it ourselves."

"That's fantastic," Kelly cried. "Remind me to let you make all my phone calls from now on."

"Anyway, I asked him to schedule it for Thursday night, when Kelly will be back, so she won't miss out on it. It's all settled, so I hope we all want to do this. We have to make it work now."

"Of course we will," Jennifer said. "It's the best idea anyone around here has had in years!"

Everyone started talking at once. There were a million plans to be made, and since Kelly was leaving for Houston the next morning, she wanted to help as much as she could. They ordered more colas and made list after list.

"We've made a pretty good start," Sue remarked. She glanced at her watch and leapt up suddenly. "Yipes, I was supposed to be home half an hour ago."

Lisa stood up also. "Can I grab a ride? Listen, Kelly, have a terrific time in Houston. I'll be thinking of you while I slave away in school."

Rochelle leaned over and gave Kelly a kiss. "Say hi to all the millionaires for me. Maybe they're tired of the high life and would want to settle down with a nice girl from New Jersey . . ."

"Yeah, sure." Kelly laughed. "Go on, get out of here. I'll see you in a few days."

Jennifer stayed behind, draining her glass. "I guess I should be going, too."

"Don't go, Jen, stay just a minute. I don't know why Eric is so late, but he's got to show up any second. You don't mind waiting with me, do you?"

"Okay, for a minute. Anyway, we ought to try to settle as many details as we can for this skating party. No offense, but Rochelle and Lisa talk better than they work. With you gone, I have a feeling it'll be me and Sue putting this whole thing together."

"You may be right. But Rochelle isn't as lazy as she pretends, and if you give Lisa something specific to do, she'll come through."

"If you say so," Jennifer said doubtfully. "But listen, I think we should . . ."

The door crashed open, and Eric Powers hurried over to their booth, bringing a breeze of cool air with him. His cheeks were flushed and his blue eyes were dark, as they always were when he was preoccupied. Kelly's heart leapt at the sight of him. He was so adorable, Kelly could hardly believe he was her boyfriend at last.

Eric slid into the booth next to Jennifer, across from Kelly. "Hi," he said softly, looking into her eyes.

"Hi, yourself," she said, gazing back. *Oh, Eric, just once I wish you'd give me a casual kiss hello, so everyone would know you were mine.* But that was the last thing Eric would do in public. He was too shy. Kelly had to be content with a long glance in which she tried to tell him how much she'd missed him that afternoon. But he was already looking away, saying hello to Jennifer, without a word of explanation for his lateness.

"Hey, Jen," he remarked, "isn't there something different about you? Did you do something to your hair?"

Jennifer reached up to make sure her butterfly clips were still in place. She'd twisted strands of dark hair away from her face and pulled new spiky bangs over her forehead—a daring hairstyle for Jennifer, who was usually so conservative.

"She looks great, doesn't she?" Kelly smiled at Eric. "So, where were you?" she asked casually. "It was getting so late, I was worried."

"I had something special to do."

"Oh, well, I have something special to tell *you*," she said.

Excited, Jennifer leaned forward, grabbing Eric's arm. "You're going to love this idea . . . Well, you tell, Kelly, it was really your idea, anyway."

"Okay." Kelly sat up straighter, trying to

decide where to begin. "We were all trying to think of a special event to plan, you know, because things are so dull right now. So, anyway, we came up with a perfect idea—the night I get back home, we're going to have a private skating party at the indoor rink—high-school kids only! We'll decorate the rink, or have a light show, or maybe even get a band."

Jennifer's mouth dropped open. "I just had a great idea. Remember those seniors who just formed a group—what's their name, the Penguins?—I'll bet they'd play for free, for the exposure."

"That's a great idea," Kelly agreed, "isn't it, Eric?"

"Sure," Eric nodded, "but I had a great idea, too. A different one, but a great one."

Playfully, Kelly put her hands on her hips. "A different idea? What's the matter with ours? Wait till you see me in the outfit I've planned, you'll forget everything else. And you'll look terrific in your jeans, so don't worry about wearing anything special."

Eric shook his head, laughing. "I wasn't worried about that. It's a great idea for some other time, but not for that particular night." He reached into his jacket pocket. "*That* night, Kelly, you and I have tickets for a Rangers' home game at Madison Square Garden. How about that?" He gave them both a proud look. "And this season the team really looks great."

Kelly gazed at him in disbelief. "A hockey game?"

"And it wasn't easy to get the tickets, believe

me. That's why I was so late in getting here. I went to three ticket outlets before I found these, and even then I had to swap with this guy to get good seats on the right night. Pretty neat, huh?"

Kelly hesitated. "But what about the skating party?"

Eric shrugged. "So we can't go skating that night, but maybe another time, Kelly." Then he looked at her more closely and his expression changed. "Kelly, is something wrong?"

"Wrong? What could be wrong? You march in here two hours late and tell me you have my life completely organized for me, ignoring the fact that I just got through making other plans. What could possibly be wrong?"

"But . . ." he began, looking puzzled. "I thought you'd be pleased about the hockey game. You know, just the two of us . . . no offense, Jen."

"And *I* thought you'd be excited about the skating party," Kelly protested. "Eric, you don't understand. It's all settled. We called the rink and reserved the date and everything. It'll really be terrific. And I'd rather go to the skating party than go to a hockey game."

"Do you realize how hard it is to get Ranger tickets?" Eric set his jaw. "I got them as a surprise for you. I thought you'd be pleased. You like hockey."

"Yes, but everyone is really excited about this party, and after all, it was my idea. I have to go, don't you see?"

"Can't you change the date and have it some other night?"

"I told you, Eric, the man at the rink agreed to *that* night. He's letting us have the place for nothing."

"But I went to so much trouble for these tickets—to surprise you. This is the hottest Rangers' season in years. And the Rangers don't rearrange their schedule for anyone's skating party."

Kelly bristled. "So I'm supposed to cancel on everyone. How are my friends going to feel? You can't just walk in here and take control of my life."

Jennifer cleared her throat as if to remind Kelly she was there, but Kelly ignored the hint. She wanted Jennifer's support.

"Come on," Eric said, "that's a little farfetched. Not to mention the fact that you haven't even said thank you."

She was astonished. "You want me to thank you for putting me in a terrible position?"

"What terrible position?"

"The position of dumping plans I've already made with my friends to go out with you. That's the worst thing a girl can do, abandoning her girlfriends for a date with a boy. Everyone hates girls who do that. I'm sorry, I can't go to that game. I have to go skating."

"And I have to use these tickets. I know half a dozen guys who'd give their right arms for these seats."

In the uncomfortable silence, the only sound was the clinking of ice cubes as Jennifer played with the straw in her drink. Kelly reached out and grabbed her wrist.

"What do you think, Jen? I can't bail out of the party, can I?"

Jennifer glanced up, and Kelly smiled at her encouragingly.

"Gee, you guys, it's been swell. But I really have to get home . . ."

"Jen, I need you here!" Only Jennifer understood how hard she'd worked to reach the point where she and Eric could be considered a steady couple. *Did I make a mistake?* Kelly wondered miserably. *With my career, I have to count on Eric to be flexible. He always was before . . . but then, that was before we were really going together.*

"I understand what you mean, but you have to consider Eric's point of view, he . . ."

"His point of view," Kelly exploded. "His point of view is that I should stab my friends in the back!"

"It's better than stabbing me in the back," Eric said stonily.

"You shouldn't stab anyone in the back," Jennifer said, as logical as ever, "but Eric has a point. You didn't even thank him, and you really are overreacting . . ."

Kelly pushed out of the booth. It was too much to take. "Some best friend," she snapped before Jennifer could finish.

Jennifer turned red, which she rarely did, and stared at her soda glass. Kelly felt a pang of remorse at having said something so stupid.

"Hey, Kelly, lay off," Eric said sharply. "She doesn't deserve that."

Kelly felt tears of self-pity well up. Her last

night home, and Eric was defending Jennifer and criticizing her! "And I don't deserve you yelling at me. Since when did I become your enemy?" Blindly, she groped for her jacket and shoulder bag. "Thanks for a wonderful farewell. I hope everyone enjoys the week while I'm away. How nice it will be for you all, telling each other how terrible I am."

"Kelly," Eric called as she slammed out of the coffee shop. "Kelly, come back here."

But she'd started to run, glad she'd worn sneakers. Home was only two miles away, and Kelly had covered half the distance before she slowed down. *Whew!* she thought. *I haven't sprinted like that since I quit the track team.* She wondered what was wrong with her, why she had caused such a scene. She wasn't usually like this. Uneasily, she wondered if Jennifer was right; could she be overreacting? But why? Why, on the night before she left, was she acting as if she wanted to drive Eric away?

Two

Kelly pushed aside her bedroom curtain for the tenth time and peered into the darkness. A pair of headlights blinked as a car turned down the street, and she felt hopeful: maybe it was Eric at last. But whoever it was drove past, not pausing at the house across the street where Eric lived. *Where could Eric be at this hour? Why isn't he home yet?* she wondered. *And where's Jen? I must have called her house ten times tonight, and nobody ever answers!*

She let the curtain drop. Her door opened quietly and her mother entered the room, a stack of freshly ironed clothes balanced on one arm.

"Goodness, Kelly, I thought you'd be asleep." Mrs. Blake dropped the pile of clothes on Kelly's bureau. "What are you doing still up? I thought you wanted to get to sleep early since your flight is first thing in the morning."

"I tried, but I'm just not sleepy, I guess."

"Is everything all right?" Kelly's mother looked tired herself. "You seemed so edgy tonight. I know you're excited about the trip, but are you sure there isn't something else wrong?"

"No, I'm just nervous about the job, I guess."

"Well, who wouldn't be?" Her mother sat on a corner of the bed. "I don't want you to worry about missing school. You proved you could handle the makeup work the last time, and after all, it's only four school days. Too bad the time difference works against you; by the time we bring you back from the airport on Thursday, there won't be much point in taking you to school. Just promise me you'll try to look at your books once or twice. I won't be unrealistic, I know it's going to be hard for you to do more than that." She sighed, her brow furrowed with concern. "I don't know, maybe we're asking too much of you . . ."

Kelly felt a rush of sympathy, almost pity, for her mother. She worried about her so much. For an instant, Kelly was tempted to admit that she was upset about Eric, but somehow she couldn't discuss that with her mother. She hated to admit her part in their fight. It was all so complicated.

"I'll be all right, Mom." She patted her mother on the back.

"I hope you won't regret this someday, Kelly. I hope you won't look back and wonder where the time went. Goodness knows you have enough to do without a modeling career, just growing up and making friends, falling in and out of love . . ."

Kelly's sympathy turned to embarrassment and she rolled her eyes. "Look, Mom, it's not like I missed my childhood! And I really should try to get some sleep now." She stretched and faked a big yawn. "Don't forget you have to get up early to take me to the airport. You'd better get to sleep, too."

"You're right, honey," her mother murmured. "Well, see you in the morning."

Kelly stared at her closed bedroom door. Her mother might be too sentimental sometimes, but she was right about one thing; it wasn't easy growing up and falling in and out of love. With a sigh she climbed into bed.

But she couldn't sleep. Now she really regretted her outburst in Campy's, and worse than that, she wasn't entirely sure why it had happened. She was right not to have given in, she was sure of that. Eric shouldn't have demanded that she drop her plans. But she should have been calmer about it, and she never should have snapped at Jennifer that way. *It must be the Houston job*, she thought. *I must be more nervous than I'd realized.*

She got out of bed and picked up the telephone in her room. Then she dialed Jennifer's number again.

There was still no answer. She felt irritated with Jennifer. Here she was, willing to apologize for her outburst in the coffee shop, and Jennifer wasn't even home to talk about it!

Kelly padded back to bed. It was hardly an

ideal way to leave home for several days, with her best friend and her boyfriend angry with her. She felt a pang of anxiety. *Jen and Eric couldn't be out together, could they? No, that's stupid.*

Feeling fidgety, Kelly drifted toward the window again. Eric knew she was leaving first thing in the morning; how could he deliberately let her go off angry? It made her wonder if he really cared about her. If you really loved someone you didn't let her go without saying good-bye.

I could try calling his house, and leave a message for him to call me in the morning. No! I shouldn't be the only one making any effort.

Intending to lie down and listen for a while for Eric's car, she fell asleep. She had a crazy mixed-up dream in which everything was scrambled together, Eric and her job in Houston. She dreamed she saw him walking with another girl, and as she tried to run after him, the dress she was modeling tangled around her legs, tripping her. It was a relief when her mother's voice woke her and she realized it was morning, and time to get ready to leave for the airport.

Paisley Gregg emptied her bottle of Perrier into a spray bottle and spritzed her face. "You know you should do this once an hour while you're flying. The pressurized cabin dehydrates your skin."

"Does it?" Kelly glanced at Paisley briefly, then continued staring at her magazine.

"Here—try it."

"Oh . . . thanks." A little self-consciously,

Kelly aimed the spray at her own face, wondering if the passenger across the aisle would think she was crazy. She handed the bottle back to Paisley.

"Hey, why so gloomy?" Paisley asked her. "You're not still feeling nauseous, are you?"

"No, no, my stomach settled down after the takeoff." Kelly flipped through the glossy pages, but her mind wasn't on the magazine.

"You can't fool me," Paisley said, the southern accent that came and went in her voice becoming more pronounced. "You're stewing about something. I know you're worried about our Houston job, but just because you've never done an assignment like this before doesn't mean you *can't* do it. Of course, informal modeling is boring—I'll never know why a designer as famous as Noireau has to do these promotional tours. Five whole days promoting 'The Total Noireau Woman.'" Paisley shook her head and sighed. "It's going to seem an eternity, I guarantee, and by the end of it you'll be so sick of Noireau makeup, Noireau perfume, and Noireau clothes you'll want to *spit* at anything European."

Kelly smiled politely. Actually, she was still thinking about Eric. Not only hadn't he called the night before, he hadn't called in the morning, either. She'd watched his house as she drove off that morning for the airport, hoping until the last minute that he might run out on the porch to say good-bye, but he hadn't.

"Paisley, didn't you do one of these trunk shows last year?"

"It seems like I've done one every year of my *life*, but, yes, last year was my first time." She pulled a copy of their itinerary from her tote bag. "We certainly have enough to do. Still, I think it could be a lot of fun."

Kelly nodded, but despite herself, she already felt a pang of homesickness. She tried to fight it down. She didn't know which was worse; nervousness about the assignment, anxiety that she'd be homesick, or fear that she'd spend her entire time away feeling sick about her fight with Eric.

Her schoolbooks were in a knapsack at her feet, and she pulled out a text. "If they keep us busy all day, and I spend my nights catching up on all this studying, I won't have a minute to myself."

Paisley gave her an astute glance. "You sound like you want that to happen."

Kelly flushed. "Not at all," she said. "Why should I want that?"

"Because you're homesick. Well, that's one thing that never bothers me," Paisley said easily. "The more traveling I do, the better I like it. Everyone's life should be like mine; out of the house and on your own as soon as you're able, that's what I say. Let's see, it's been just about three years that I've been living in the Belvedere Professional Women's Hotel, ever since I was fourteen, and I swear, I never felt *one bit* homesick in all that time."

Kelly didn't say what she was thinking: that Paisley must not have left much of a home behind if she never once felt homesick for it. Ever since she'd met Paisley through the FLASH! agency, Kelly had been dying to know about the girl's personal life. But Paisley never volunteered a bit of information about her family, and some instinct told Kelly that it might cost her Paisley's friendship if she were to ask questions.

So she tolerated Paisley's mysteries. It was worth it, she felt, glancing around the plane at the other models. There was Margaretta, a buxom redhead she'd worked with before, and several other models she recognized from other agencies; but no one except Paisley had ever made a real attempt to be Kelly's friend.

"Who are you looking at?" Paisley asked.

"Just looking to see who else came along," Kelly muttered.

"Don't bother with that bunch. They're all jealous of you, anyway."

"I'm sure they're not."

"Don't be so sure. You've already gotten more good assignments than most of them put together—and you're still a newcomer."

"There's no reason for them to be jealous."

"Ha!" Paisley snorted. "Look, I admit even I was a little suspicious of you at first; Miss Young and Innocent. And there was Meg Dorian, head of FLASH! herself, bragging about what a star you were going to be. It's a good thing you messed up a lot, or I would have *believed* you were Little Miss Perfect."

"I didn't mess up, *you* got me in trouble," Kelly protested. It had happened on their first job together, a runway show for a charity benefit. Paisley had talked Kelly into staying to dance after the modeling ended, and Kelly had nearly been caught by Meg.

"You got us *both* into trouble," Paisley insisted, "until I showed you the ropes. But that's okay, it's kind of fun to have a friend in this business. Everyone is such a cutthroat. You know, Blake, I'm really beginning to like you."

Kelly grinned. She was becoming quite fond of Paisley herself. The tall, striking girl had a personality as vivid as her vibrant red hair and flashing dark eyes.

"You know, Paisley," she remarked idly, "your southern drawl seems to have taken on a hint of Texas ever since we got on this plane."

"Has it?" Paisley asked innocently. "How funny, I just can't imagine why."

"Anyway, I'm glad you and I are roommates this week. It's a perfect arrangement for both of us. You're grounded, so you can help me study at night, and that way everyone will be happy."

"Me help you study?" Paisley laughed helplessly. "Listen, there's only one thing you need to study, and that's Texas money. Now, here's the way it works in Houston: oil money is strictly new money, usually corporate-executive types. Rich, but boring. Cattle money is older money, more respectable and socially prominent. But the oldest money, the kind that comes with a social pedigree a mile long, is cotton money. You find yourself a rich boy from a cotton family, and you've got it made for life." Paisley leaned back in her seat, a dreamy expression on her face. "What do you think a cotton man looks like, anyway?"

"Wait a minute," Kelly said in a warning tone. "Aren't you forgetting what Meg said?"

"Oh, Meg says lots of things I don't listen to."

"Paisley, Meg Dorian gave you an ultimatum: shape up on this assignment, or say good-bye to FLASH! One word about you chasing Texas men, old money or new, and you'll never work for Meg again. And Meg is the best."

"Oh, come on. She doesn't scare me."

"Paisley . . ."

"Okay, okay, I hear you, but don't get carried away. Meg simply warned me not to go around pestering people with my original fashion designs. I didn't even bring my portfolio with me, despite all the millionaires I might meet who could set me up in business."

"That's a relief."

"And furthermore, Meg is only worried that I might get into trouble. But I can have a few casual dates without getting in trouble."

"You can't *breathe* without getting in trouble, Paisley! Please, for my sake, take it easy, okay? Think of me; if you got fired, how would I get along by myself?"

"That's true. You do need constant supervision. You've got a lot to learn, girl."

"Yes, and you need to stay on Meg's good side. It won't be so bad. The two of us together can still have lots of fun."

Paisley's eyes lit up. "Together—then you'll double-date with me?"

"Paisley! I wasn't talking about dating at all! Get serious a minute. Everyone at FLASH! knows about the lecture Meg gave you! No more staying out all night, no more chasing men and flirting . . . and she means it this time. If she catches you up to your old tricks, you're finished. This is serious."

"Oh, all she said was that she didn't like me staying out all night because I get bags under my eyes, and that just *ruins* my photos. But we're not posing for photos this week, it's all live modeling, and a cover-up stick does wonders for my eyes."

"Paisley, you're impossible. I give up." Kelly opened her textbook, but she couldn't study. She kept thinking about Eric.

Suddenly Paisley put her hand over the page. Kelly looked up, startled. "I know schoolwork can be boring, but, honey, you're reading that book upside down. You really are nervous about this job! Here I thought you were getting used to things, but you're still an amateur."

"I am not."

"You're positively green around the gills. Sick to your stomach, aren't you, butterflies and all."

"I'm not even thinking about this assignment," Kelly exclaimed. "I'm upset because Eric and I had a fight last night. Well, not really a fight. More of a misunderstanding. And I was completely willing to make up and say I was sorry, but he never called. He hadn't even gotten home by the time I went to sleep last night. I hoped that this morning he'd come over or call or something. But nothing—a big fat zero."

Paisley gave an all-knowing nod. "Uh-huh. And you're wasing your time worrying about that?"

"You wouldn't worry, Paisley?"

"Not me. I wouldn't wait around for any guy to apologize, not unless he was really worth waiting for. Be realistic! Eric Powers has done nothing but string you along, expecting you to wait while he fools around with his old girlfriend."

"But he broke up with Clarissa, I told you. We've been going together for real. Things have been just the way I always wanted them."

Paisley raised an eyebrow. "Have they? And I suppose you had to give up seeing Alex Hawkins."

"Alex and I are just friends, so I didn't have to give him up."

"Right. I approve of that—no use throwing away perfectly good merchandise. You're smart to keep Alex hanging around. Your only mistake was to make any promises to Eric. You should be free, Kelly! Think of the boys out there, willing and waiting to be discovered by Kelly Blake. You haven't given yourself half a chance. You could have a whole new life. You're not just some silly high-school girl anymore. Take advantage of it. Let yourself be seen, get around. There are a lot of guys out there with tons more to offer than a hometown boy like Eric can."

"I'm not looking for anyone else. It's just that Eric really makes me mad sometimes. Ever since he broke up with Clarissa, he's started assuming I agree with him on everything, no matter where, when, or what it is." She gave an exasperated sigh. "Sometimes I even wonder if I did the right thing, saying I'd go with him exclusively."

"You see?"

"Whatever happened to 'happily ever after,'" Kelly complained. "I thought having a steady boyfriend was supposed to end all my problems." She let out a long sigh. "Maybe we're just not right for each other. Maybe I don't even know what's best for me."

"Now you're talking. I could have told you that."

"Sometimes I find myself wishing he was different, more easygoing, and then I hate myself. I thought Eric was exactly like me and that he'd be perfect. He isn't exactly like me at all!"

"Of course not. Your whole *life* is changing in ways Eric would never dream about. Eric is a nice boy from a nice family just like yours, who lives in a nice house just like yours in the same neighborhood. That used to be fine, but you can do better than that now."

"Maybe you're right. Maybe I don't need someone like me at all, maybe what I really need is someone completely *different* from me." She tossed the textbook under her seat. "Maybe I just expected too much from Eric."

"No, you didn't," Paisley said eagerly. "You didn't expect *enough.* Listen to me, there are a million boys better for you than Eric, and I'll bet one of them is in Houston, right now!"

"That's ridiculous. But maybe I shouldn't have put all my hopes on one boy."

Just then the stewardess came down the aisle, telling them to fasten their seat belts. "We are now beginning our descent into Houston Intercontinental Airport," the pilot's voice came over the loudspeaker. "We have a beautiful, sunny day, with the temperature presently at 61 degrees. Thank you for flying with us, and enjoy your stay in the Lone Star State."

Outside the window, the Houston skyline suddenly appeared, and Kelly felt a surge of nervous anticipation. Her life was changing so fast; she really wasn't the ordinary teenager she used to be. Paisley was right about that. Was she right about Eric, too? Was there really someone out there, right this very minute, better for her than Eric?

Three

The bellboy unlocked the door, picked up their bags, and led them into the suite.

"Now *this* is living!" Paisley pulled open the curtains, approving of the spectacular view of downtown Houston.

"It's the best location in town," the bellboy agreed. "We have it all, right here in the Galleria—restaurants, shopping, a health club, even an Olympic-sized indoor skating rink."

Startled, Kelly looked up. "Skating rink! That's really bizarre. That's exactly what Eric and I fought over, going to a party at the skating rink! Maybe it's some kind of weird omen."

Paisley frowned at her. "Not in front of *him*," she whispered. Grandly, she pulled a five-dollar bill out of her pocketbook and flapped it at the bellboy. "Thanks, that will be all for now," she said.

The bellboy's face lit up, and he bowed slightly before backing out the door.

Kelly gaped. "Five dollars for taking our suitcases off the elevator?"

"This is Texas, everything's bigger here. Now he thinks we're a couple of big shots. It's worth the money."

"Well, I'd better split it with you." Kelly opened her wallet, drawing out two dollar bills and some change.

"When I want your money I'll ask you for it," Paisley said. "Save it for that big college education your folks have planned for you."

"Okay, but I feel funny letting you pay for things like that when we both make good money modeling."

"Forget it. You'll pay me back some other way."

Kelly flung her suitcase onto her bed and opened it. Suddenly, she let out a cry of surprise.

Paisley stared. "What on earth is the matter?"

"Look at what my mother stuck in my suitcase." Trying to hide her embarrassment, Kelly held up a heart-shaped picture frame. Inside was a photograph of the Blake family: Kelly, her mother, her stepfather, Hal, and her half sister, Tina, gathered around the living room fireplace. There was an inscription painted on the ceramic frame: Home Is Where the Heart Is.

"My mother's not very sophisticated sometimes," Kelly said apologetically.

Paisley examined the photograph. "The wholesome all-American family," she quipped. There was a strange expression on her face, and Kelly wasn't sure if Paisley was making fun of her or if she was actually envious of Kelly's close family. It was hard to tell with Paisley.

Glancing down, Kelly realized there was something else stuck in between the clothes and toiletries in her suitcase—she would know that telltale gleam anywhere, after years of summer camp and slumber parties. Paisley would *really* laugh at her now. Casually, she tried to close her suitcase, but Paisley had already seen inside.

"What's that? Isn't that something wrapped in tinfoil?"

"No," Kelly protested, trying to block Paisley's view. "There's nothing else in there."

But Paisley shoved Kelly aside. She took a square, foil-wrapped package out of the suitcase. "It's squishy, and it smells like chocolate. What is this?"

Kelly sighed. "I guess it might be brownies," she finally admitted. "Really, my mom forgets I'm not twelve anymore. She always baked something for me when I went away. I guess she can't break the habit."

"These are really homemade brownies?" Paisley hesitated. "Do you think there are enough for the two of us?"

Kelly laughed. "Sure. We'll save them for later—a midnight snack, okay?"

Carefully, she tucked the package into the tiny refrigerator in their living room. Suddenly Kelly felt glad her mother was so sentimental.

"Well, don't just sit there, Kelly, hurry up and

finish unpacking," Paisley said. "We have work to do today."

The Galleria was the most impressive shopping center Kelly had ever seen, more like a small city than a mall. Besides having two luxury hotels, Loretta Crabtree, the supervisor in charge of the Noireau promotion, told the models proudly, the Galleria had not one, not two, but five major department stores. Not to mention the dozens of chic, ultra-expensive boutiques; everything from Tiffany to Gucci. All in all, there were over 250 businesses, nineteen restaurants, and most unbelievable of all, an indoor skating rink, Olympic size!

Loretta gave them a quick tour and then showed them to the dressing room which, up until that morning, had simply been an immense, opulent powder room for shoppers. Now, a velvet rope declared the marble and gold-trimmed lounge, with its ample makeup tables and comfortable chairs, off limits to anyone not involved in the week's fashion events. They quickly changed into the outfits they would wear for the afternoon's informal modeling.

"Remember, girls, when you wear a Noireau creation you are the personification of the Noireau woman," Loretta told them.

Kelly wondered if Loretta was the personification of the Noireau woman. Loretta's auburn hair was piled high and lacquered into place, and her deep red mouth was drawn on precisely. Her look was certainly different from Kelly's own ideal.

But even so, Kelly had to admit it was very stylish—and eye-catching.

Loretta was busy spraying perfume over Paisley's hair, ignoring the indignant look Paisley gave her. "This is just the finishing touch you need. All week, you will be privileged to wear Noireau, smell Noireau, think Noireau." She stepped back, her high heels clicking on the tile floor, then nodded in approval. "Your pale skin is perfect for that makeup. The Noireau woman is not the hearty type. Beautiful, yes, illusive, yes. Seductively pale, but not innocently pale."

"Seductive my eye," Paisley muttered. "I look sickly in this pancake makeup."

Kelly shot her a warning glance. "You do look dramatic," she said quickly. "And I'm sure Loretta knows the Noireau look better than we do."

"You look pretty Noireau yourself," Paisley grumbled.

"One final look at all of you," Loretta ordered, clapping her hands. A dozen models lined up. Kelly looked at them all, trying to be professional in her appraisal. The girls were all types, all nationalities, but she had to admit each was equally stunning. There would be stiff competition in the contest for the Miss Noireau contract. She really had her work cut out for her.

"I didn't know there would be so many of us," Paisley muttered. "And from all over the world. I didn't realize this was such a big deal."

Loretta overheard, and frowned severely. "This is the biggest 'deal' of all! At the end of this week, just one of you lovely ladies will have the honor of being named Miss Noireau. Why, it's more than an honor, it's a privilege!"

"It's a bore," Paisley whispered.

"That lucky young woman will be seen world-wide, her face and figure the symbol of international beauty and flair. It means fame, it means fortune, it means . . ."

"Putting up with you," Paisley muttered.

Kelly elbowed Paisley in the side. The last thing she wanted was to get Loretta angry at them. She was serious about winning the contest. Besides, if Loretta told Meg Dorian that Paisley was misbehaving, it might be the end of Paisley's career.

"All right, girls," Loretta called for silence. "You have all seen the plaza area. You are to wander out among the tables, modeling the clothes in a gracious, yet informal manner. Those weary shoppers need their tea and refreshments after shopping all day, and some may be tired and cranky, but remember, these ladies are our best customers. They are wealthy, important people. Otherwise they wouldn't be here. Be friendly but dignified. Tell them about your outfit if you are asked, but above all be natural. And remember, even if you think they are overweight and middle-aged, each one of those ladies thinks a Noireau will make her slim and youthful. Do not do anything to hint otherwise. Remember, girls, you are all Noireau's ambassadors. Now go out there and make me proud!"

Smiles plastered on their faces, the models drifted into the plaza, strolling among the women sipping tea, trying to look casual yet dignified, natural yet dramatic. Kelly's three-piece suit was cut from very luxurious wool, but it was also very warm wool. It wasn't long before she was looking casual, dignified, and sweaty. She decided to take a breather and ducked behind a marble wall to flap her suit jacket to get a breeze.

"Another deserter!" Paisley greeted her, already leaning against the wall, well out of sight of the plaza. "Welcome to my secret hiding place. How do you like informal modeling? Lots of fun, isn't it?"

"I just wish they'd turn on the air-conditioning," Kelly said. "I'm suffocating in this suit; I'll never make it through the day." She kicked off her shoes and stretched her toes, sighing in relief.

"Tell me about it," Paisley said. "And I hate the way we look. These skirts are so narrow. I can barely walk in mine."

"Actually, I think they look kind of nice," Kelly told her, keeping her voice low. "Not like our own style, of course, but kind of ladylike and, I don't know, sort of French."

Paisley gave her a scornful glance. "French—if it's French to suffer, then I'm very French. My feet are killing me; I'll be totally crippled in another hour. I *told* Loretta I hate high heels, but she made me wear them anyway."

"The Noireau woman never complains," Kelly quipped.

"That's easy for you to say; that color is terrific on you. I don't know why I got stuck with the bright green outfit. Didn't Loretta ever hear that redheads shouldn't wear green? I feel like a Christmas tree."

"Really, Paisley, you look good. I like that look on you. In fact, you ought to dress that way more often."

"Ugh—in a prim-and-proper suit, with ropes of pearls and all these jangly bracelets? Loretta would look at home in this outfit, but not me. I can't wait to get to our room and put my jeans on."

Kelly nodded. "I agree with you there."

"Uh-oh," Paisley suddenly said. "Get back—here comes the Dragon Lady herself."

"Who?"

"Loretta." Paisley yanked Kelly farther behind the wall. "It's okay, she didn't see us; she went over to that table by the fountain. Look at her, gushing over that woman with the diamonds. She makes me sick. Think Noireau, smell Noireau. Let's just stay here until she's gone."

"That's fine with me," Kelly said, rubbing her sore toes.

"I'm so bored." Paisley yawned. "It's tragic, isn't it, all these millionaires and not one interesting man among them."

"Paisley—we came here to work, not to meet men. Remember what Meg said."

"I remember."

"Good. No men, no trouble." Kelly peered around the wall. "I don't see Loretta anymore. Let's go back out." She slipped her feet into her shoes and rebuttoned her jacket. "Come on, before Loretta notices us missing."

"Yes, that's a *wonderful* idea," Paisley said,

taking Kelly's arm. "Let's get out there and show them what the Noireau woman is all about."

Kelly looked up sharply. Paisley's voice had suddenly taken on an exaggerated southern drawl, the way it always did when Paisley spotted adventure. And with Paisley, adventure meant trouble.

"Paisley," she warned, "we only have an hour and a half to go. Please, let's make it a nice, calm, peaceful time."

"Why, Kelly, you sweet little thing, whatever makes you so suspicious? A calm, peaceful time is exactly what I had in mind."

Kelly followed Paisley's gaze. The first thing she saw were two ten-gallon hats, the kind the heroes always wore in old cowboy movies.

"Oh, no," Kelly groaned. "Here comes trouble."

"I just want to take a little look at those hats and boots," Paisley assured her.

"It's not the hats and boots I'm worried about," Kelly muttered, "it's what's in them. Paisley, please—don't start any trouble."

Paisley laughed, a bright trilling peal of laughter. "Honey, this won't be any trouble at all. Why, it'll be as easy as taking candy from a baby. I think I'll take the tall blond one. That cute little dark-haired guy is more your type."

Kelly grabbed for Paisley's arm, hoping to hold her back and talk some sense into her, but Paisley was already slinking toward her prey.

"Paisley, wait, come back here," Kelly hissed. "Remember what Meg Dorian told you."

"Why, Kelly, I'm surprised at you. Loretta

wants us to mingle with the guests. I'm only doing my job."

Kelly set her shoulders and took a deep breath. Paisley had halted, one hand on her hip, striking a dramatic pose in the sexy green dress. The blond that Paisley had picked as her target took one look and stopped dead in his tracks. Kelly wouldn't have been surprised if he'd whistled.

"How do, ma'am. Let me introduce myself. Gerard Manfred Offenbacher at your service. But you can call me Skip."

"Skip—is that a cowboy nickname?" Paisley gave him a frank once-over, seeming to approve of what she saw.

Kelly, however, was not impressed by his stocky build, curly light hair, sideburns that no one in New Jersey would be caught dead wearing, a bushy mustache that made her cringe, and the ridiculous ten-gallon hat. He swept the hat off his head and winked at Paisley.

"Is Skip a cowboy nickname? Well, yes and no. My great-granddaddy was one of the first meat-packers in the state of Texas. Put the Offenbacher name on the map, you might say. We don't rope 'em, but we slice 'em and pack 'em and ship 'em."

"That sounds thrilling," Paisley said.

That sounds disgusting, Kelly thought.

"I love your hat." Paisley moved closer. "I didn't know anyone actually wore hats like that anymore. I didn't even know they still made them."

"They make them, all right," Skip drawled, "and this here is a custom-made version, genuine

Texas-style. And look at these boots—hand-tooled of fine Spanish leather."

"Are they custom-made, too?"

"Yep," Skip said proudly. "They cost a pretty penny, but I always say, money well spent is money worth spendin'."

"I always say that myself." Paisley gazed at him thoughtfully. "You know, I don't think the name 'Skip' suits you. Somehow, it doesn't sound right. I think I'll just call you Gerard. It's much more dignified."

Gerard's eyelids blinked rapidly in surprise. "No one ever said that to me before, but you know, I think you're right. Skip does sound a little undignified."

"Absolutely," Paisley purred. "You know, Gerard, I've never been to Texas before, but you're exactly what I imagined a genuine western cowboy to be."

"And you seem like a lively little filly yourself. What did you say your name was?"

Paisley hesitated, glancing at Kelly, who gave her a stern look.

"Why, I'm Kelly Blake," Paisley said coolly.

Four

Kelly stared at Paisley in horror. Were her ears playing tricks on her, or had Paisley really introduced herself as "Kelly Blake"? She blurted, "Excuse us for a minute, Gerard," and pulled Paisley aside.

"Paisley, what do you think you're doing? Why did you use my name?"

"You should know why," Paisley retorted. "You've been telling me all day that Meg will kill me if she finds out I'm dating anyone on this assignment. But I certainly don't intend to let a catch like Gerard get away from me just because Meg's in a snit."

"Meg in a snit!" Kelly shut her eyes in disbelief. "Paisley, Meg has every right to be angry with you! She owns FLASH! If she wants you to wear green bananas in your ears she can make you do it. Paisley, be reasonable! Drop this thing with Gerard before you get started. It isn't worth the risk."

"What risk?" Paisley gave Gerard a little wave. "Meg said she didn't want to hear about Paisley Gregg fooling around in Houston. She didn't say one word about Kelly Blake. So if I use your name, all she might hear is that Kelly Blake is dating Gerard Manfred Offenbacher. Nothing terrible is going to happen to either of us, don't you see?"

"I see that you've lost your mind," Kelly said. "You don't honestly believe you can go around calling yourself by my name, do you?"

"Why not?"

"Why not," Kelly sputtered. "Why not— because it's . . . it's crazy, that's why not!"

Paisley sighed impatiently. "You can't come up with one good reason why it won't work, can you?"

"Paisley, we're going to be working here for five whole days. Loretta knows our real names, the other models know our real names, and someone's bound to call you 'Paisley' in front of Gerard. Or are you planning to go into hiding?"

"Oh, that's simple. I won't let Gerard meet me around here, that's all. So you see, there isn't any reason why I can't get away with it. It's a very simple plan: I just call myself Kelly Blake, and I go out with Gerard. And I behave myself."

Kelly groaned, but Paisley ignored her. "Yes, I behave myself. But if by any chance anyone *does* hear any little rumors, they'll be about Kelly

Blake, not Paisley Gregg. It's completely fool-proof."

"Oh, fine, so my name gets dragged through the mud, and I get a bad reputation."

"Oh, come on, Kelly," Paisley scoffed, "no one would ever believe you did anything wild. Not Miss Goody Two-Shoes."

"Don't call me that," Kelly snapped.

"Why not? Everyone at FLASH! does. You're so prim and proper."

"That's not true," Kelly protested. "I got into trouble the first time I met you, when we borrowed those designer dresses at the charity ball. Meg would've killed me if she'd found out!"

"But Meg didn't find out, so you didn't really get into trouble," Paisley pointed out.

"Well, how about the time I messed up that TV commercial—that was really bad news."

"That was pathetic," Paisley agreed, "but it wasn't the same as getting into trouble. You just got fired."

Kelly glanced over at Gerard's table. He smiled and beckoned to the girls, and she gave a loud sigh.

Paisley shook her head impatiently. "No, you'll have to face it, Kelly, you never take any real risks. I'm not telling you to go out and run wild for no reason," she added hastily, seeing Kelly about to protest. "All I'm saying is, you have a clean record with Meg Dorian. You could date any guy you wanted and nothing at all would happen. But if I so much as *look* at a guy, Meg blows her top. It really isn't fair."

"It's fair if you deserve it," Kelly insisted. But

she was bluffing; secretly, she was afraid Paisley was right. She wasn't always adventurous, and sometimes, especially when Paisley was around, she felt positively dull.

"Please, Kelly, give me a chance. It won't hurt you."

"I don't know," she said doubtfully. "It gives me the creeps to let you use my name. I don't know why."

"It doesn't bother me at all for you to use my name—which you'll have to do if I'm going to be Kelly Blake," Paisley added quickly before Kelly could protest. "But make up your mind fast, because Gerard looks impatient, and I don't want to mess this up."

"Well . . ."

Just then someone tapped Kelly on the shoulder. Annoyed, she turned and found herself staring into a pair of dark eyes. They belonged to Gerard's friend, who removed his ridiculous ten-gallon hat and actually bowed. She would have laughed out loud, but his grave expression stopped her.

Kelly hadn't really paid attention to him before, but now, with his hat off, she saw that he was really good-looking, very dramatic in fact, with his flashing dark eyes and jet black hair. She realized she was staring, and she pulled her eyes away, feeling pleased and then annoyed that she was pleased.

"Excuse me," Gerard's friend said, "but, uh, my name is Chad Renfrew. I know you don't know me or Gerard, but if it helps any, I'd just like to say that Gerard and I have been friends since the second grade, and the Offenbachers are a fine old Texas family. He's completely respectable. Why, if you don't believe me, you can even check with Miss Crabtree. She's the one who invited us here today. She belongs to the same country club as Gerard and I, and she's known both of us for years. In fact, I'd feel better if you did ask her, she'd probably be happy to vouch for us both." Chad lifted a hand to signal to Loretta.

"No, don't do that," Paisley said quickly. "I mean, you don't have to do that right now, does he, Paisley? Paisley?"

"Huh?" Kelly gaped stupidly.

"I said, *Paisley*, that we don't need Loretta to vouch for Chad and Gerard. We can ask her ourselves, later. You and I can ask her. Me"—she pointed to herself—"Kelly Blake, and you"—she pointed to Kelly—"Paisley Gregg."

"Now wait a minute, I didn't . . ." Kelly started to say, but Chad put a hand on her arm.

"Excuse me, Miss Paisley, I don't mean to be rude or anything, but haven't I seen you somewhere before? I guess an important model like you has her face in lots of magazines, but still— there's something about you . . ." He trailed off, staring at Kelly openly.

Kelly had been about to say there had been a misunderstanding; she wasn't Paisley Gregg at all, she was Kelly Blake, and the real Paisley was just playing a little joke. But something stopped her. Maybe it was the way Chad looked at her so intently, but without making her feel the least bit embarrassed. Maybe it was the quaint, old-fashioned way he had tipped his hat that made her feel intrigued by this strange boy.

She found herself staring at Chad with a silly grin on her face, and immediately, he smiled back at her. She liked the way his eyes took her in as if he couldn't get enough of her. They were such nice eyes . . .

With a shock she suddenly remembered her going-away party in Campy's, and what Rochelle had said: Across a room you see a stranger in a cowboy hat . . . your eyes meet, and something electric crackles in the air. . . .

"Paisley, Paisley! Are you okay?"

Kelly realized Chad was speaking to her. She flushed and laughed lightly. "Oh, I'm fine. It must be your Texas accent, it, uh, my name sounds so different, the way you pronounce it." Chad would think her a complete idiot, and she realized she wanted him to like her.

Chad looked abashed. "I guess I do sound pretty funny to an eastern girl like you."

"Oh, no, that's not true," Kelly said. "But Paisley is . . . just my modeling name. I mean, I use it all the time now, but . . . Oh, never mind."

Chad grinned. "Anything you say, Sugar. Mind if I call you Sugar?"

Sugar? Kelly thought, squirming. *Well, anything's better than being called Paisley and not recognizing my own name. Wait a minute, what am I thinking? Am I actually going along with this crazy scheme to switch identities?*

Chad was waiting for her answer, so Kelly forced a smile. "Oh, no, you can call me Sugar."

Gerard took one of Paisley's hands in his huge paw. "As long as we're givin' nicknames, I think Kelly ought to have one too."

"Good idea," Kelly said. "It would be mean to leave Pai—I mean, to leave Kelly out of things. She ought to have a Texas nickname, too. In fact, if anyone deserves a new name, *she* does."

Gerard looked immensely pleased. "Let me think of it—just a minute now . . ." He scowled, his big features bunched together as he concentrated. "Um, no . . . uh, how 'bout—nope, that won't do. I know, I've got it—I'll call you Red." He smiled expectantly.

"Uh, if you don't mind, Gerard," Paisley said sweetly, "Red is such a . . . well, a kind of *obvious* name for a redhead, don't you think?"

"Shoot, maybe it is at that." Gerard looked crestfallen. "Can you think of some other name I could call you?"

"Why don't you call me Sunny," Paisley said before Kelly could come up with any wisecracks. "Everyone always says what a sunny personality I have."

"Oh, we certainly do," Kelly muttered.

"Then Sugar and Sunny it is," Chad declared triumphantly. "That makes the two of you official Texas girls."

"Let's shake on it," Paisley exclaimed. They shook hands all around. Chad held on to Kelly's hand a little longer than necessary, fixing his eyes on her so intently that she felt herself blushing.

"Goodness," Paisley exclaimed, "there's Loretta heading this way, and we've been standing here chatting instead of circulating in the crowd.

Come on, Sugar, we'd better move." She pulled at Kelly's arm.

Gerard laughed. "Don't you go worryin' about that, I can fix things with Loretta. Chad told you, she knows my family. Here, do you want me to buy that dress you're wearin'? Would that make Loretta feel better about your spendin' so much time with me?" He reached into a pocket and pulled out a checkbook.

"That wouldn't hurt," Paisley chirped.

"We don't want you to buy anything," Kelly told Gerard hurriedly. "And don't even mention us to Loretta, okay, Gerard?"

"Well, sure," Gerard said slowly, "but why not? Especially as I intend to ask Sunny here out on a date. I can see you while you're workin' here, can't I, Sunny?"

"Why, of course, Gerard. Don't you dare think otherwise, not even for a minute."

"Fine, she'll date you," Kelly said, anxious to get away before Loretta came over and spilled the beans about who was who. "You can call her later tonight. Come on, uh, Sunny—we'd better go."

"How about tomorrow night? I'll meet you right here at eight o'clock," Gerard said.

"Better make that nine o'clock," Paisley told him. "We have to do a fashion show tomorrow night from six to eight."

"But you're doin' one now," Gerard said, looking confused.

"No, sweetie, this is informal modeling. We do this today and all day tomorrow, but tomorrow night is a formal job, with a runway and commentary and everything."

Chad looked surprised. "That's a pretty heavy schedule, isn't it?"

"Not for a model. Actually, I think photographic sessions are harder," Kelly cut in. "Did you think modeling was easy?"

"I never thought much about it," Chad admitted.

"Most people don't," Paisley assured him, "but let me tell you—it's hard work."

"I admire that," Chad said. "I admire anyone who works hard—I know I sure do."

"Oh? Exactly what kind of work do you do, Chad?" Paisley smiled sweetly. Kelly was afraid she would ask him his bank balance next.

"He can tell us all about his work some other time," Kelly said hastily. "Meanwhile, we have our own job to do. Come on, Pai—Sunny."

Chad frowned. "Wait a minute, Sugar, you'll come tomorrow, too, won't you? Nine o'clock, right here?"

"Well, I . . ." She watched Loretta advancing on them.

"Please," he said insistently.

"I'm not sure I . . ." Loretta was bearing down on them at full speed now. "Of course, sure I'll go out with you, Chad. But we've *got* to go now."

Dragging Paisley by the hand, she plunged into the center of the plaza where the tables were more numerous and where most of the shoppers were gathered.

Three women exclaimed over Kelly's outfit and asked her to stop and show them how it looked with the jacket opened.

"Uh, it opens like this." Kelly held the edges of the jacket apart and turned around once or twice.

"A double date, just what I was hoping we'd do," Paisley exclaimed as the women asked Kelly to walk away and then come toward them again.

"That looks easy to move in," one of the women remarked.

"Yes, it's very comfortable," Kelly answered dutifully. "I'm not sure I *want* to go on this date," she hissed under her breath to Paisley.

"Why not? Chad is adorable, if you like that slim, wiry type. Personally, I prefer a more solid guy like Gerard. Gerard—even his name sounds substantial."

Kelly ignored the woman who was fingering the soft wool of the suit and stared at Paisley in surprise. "Substantial, solid . . . Since when do you care about those things?"

"Don't be silly, I care now. Would I go out with him if I didn't? And I'd go out with him even if I had to use my real name and Meg heard about it and told me to leave FLASH! forever."

"I don't believe you. Nothing could be that important. You love modeling. Your career means everything to you!"

"Apparently not," Paisley said gaily.

"But you don't even know Gerard—you just met him, you barely said ten sentences to him."

"That's the way romance is sometimes, it happens"—Paisley snapped her fingers in the air—"just like that!"

One of the women at the table nodded. "That's the way it was with me and my first husband. Love at first sight." She sighed.

Kelly hardly heard her. "You can't expect me to take this seriously, Paisley. Are you sure you're not just saying this because Gerard seems to be . . . well-off?"

"Loaded, you mean. Naturally that has something to do with it, but not everything. Gerard is different. I've dated lots of rich guys, spoiled and high-strung rich guys. Gerard seems . . . reliable. The kind of guy you can really count on, the kind who'll always be there for you."

"Just like my first husband." The woman at the table sighed again.

"I've never heard you talk like this before." Kelly frowned thoughtfully. "Maybe I'm being too harsh. Maybe going out with Gerard would be good for you."

"I know it will," Paisley told her. "But I'm going to see him anyway, no matter what you say."

"Good for you," said the woman at the table.

Paisley smiled at her, then turned to Kelly. "And just think of all the fun we'll have together this week, you and me and Gerard and Chad! We'll turn Houston upside down."

"Hold on, I know I said I'd go out with Chad, but I could change my mind by tomorrow night." Kelly began buttoning up her suit jacket as if that settled the matter.

"Why would you do that?" Paisley stared at her, aghast. "Sometimes I don't understand you at all. What in the world is wrong with Chad?"

"It's not so much that anything's wrong with Chad . . ." Involuntarily, Kelly remembered Chad's dark eyes. "There are a million reasons why I can't go out with him," she said curtly.

"Name one."

"It's a false relationship, a charade. He doesn't even know my real name."

"Big deal," Paisley scoffed. "What's a name, anyway? So he calls you by a harmless nickname—there's nothing wrong with that. Names don't matter at all." She glanced at the woman at the table, who nodded in agreement.

"But it isn't right to lie to Chad, and it isn't right to date him when I'm still involved with Eric . . ."

"Aha!" Paisley said in triumph. "Eric—I knew it, you're having second thoughts about *him* again. You said he let you down; you said you weren't even sure he was the right guy for you; you said he was narrow-minded and stubborn."

"Just like my first husband," the woman at the table exclaimed. "I had to divorce him."

"You said he didn't give you enough freedom and he was threatened by your career," Paisley continued.

"I didn't say all that," Kelly protested.

"But it's true. Admit it."

Paisley waited for Kelly's answer.

"But I'm not sure I'd be going out with Chad for the right reasons. Maybe I'd just be using him to get back at Eric."

"That's as good a reason as any. What's wrong with doing a little comparison shopping? What if Eric is wrong for you? Do you want to wait around for years to find that out, like this woman here?" Paisley pointed at the woman at the table.

"Don't do it, honey," the woman said. "Your friend is right. You're young and pretty; don't settle for the first guy to come along."

Actually, Kelly thought, there was some sense in what the woman was saying. Still, she hesitated.

"You know what I think," Paisley finally said. "I think you really do like Chad. I think you're attracted to him, and that scares you, because you have some warped notion about being loyal to your hometown boyfriend, who didn't even call to say good-bye before you went away. I think you like Chad more than you're willing to admit, but you're just too stubborn to say so because . . ."

"Because what?" Kelly said irritably.

"Because you're in a rut. You don't know how to take the teeniest little risk."

Kelly gave her a sour glance. "You don't know what you're talking about," she insisted.

"Then you won't go out with Chad?"

"I didn't say that. Maybe I will go out with him. But not because of anything you said. Just because . . . because it seems like the only proper thing to do. After all, I've already accepted."

"You like him," Paisley crowed. "I knew she did," she said to the woman at the table. "You should see these two together; they'll make a gorgeous couple!"

The woman put down her drink and burst into applause. The two other women laughed heartily. Kelly gave them a weak smile.

Five

The second afternoon of informal modeling went smoothly. Loretta hadn't said anything to either Kelly or Paisley about their flirting, but Kelly was still vastly relieved that Gerard and Chad hadn't returned to the Galleria on Sunday.

She met up with Paisley as the session was winding down. "No sign of them," she said. "Let's head for the dressing room."

"I don't think Loretta even noticed yesterday," Paisley said. "But just the same, from now on, I intend to keep my record clean. I've got to be on my best behavior so nothing interferes with my plans for Gerard."

They made their way across the wide plaza to the luxurious powder room which had been reserved for the models for the week, nodding cheerfully at women who admired their glamorous outfits.

"And what exactly *are* your plans for poor Gerard?"

"Don't worry, nothing sinister. I just intend to dazzle him with my high spirits and sense of fun—good grief, don't turn around!"

"What's the matter?"

"Oh, no! This is terrible—this is worse than I ever imagined. It's already over! How could Meg do this to me?"

"Paisley, what are you talking about? Why shouldn't I turn around? What's going on?"

"A spy! Meg sent a spy to check up on me."

"A spy?" Kelly burst out laughing.

"I've got a good mind to go over there and tear her notes up into little pieces and throw them right in her face!"

"What notes? Is someone actually taking notes?" Despite Paisley's protests, Kelly turned around. Two tables away a sleek-looking woman stared at Paisley intently as she scribbled into a notebook. Kelly's mouth dropped open. "I don't believe it—there *is* someone watching you and taking notes. A real spy!"

Michelle Chalfonte, a young model from the French division of FLASH!, heard them and snickered. "You do not know who that 'spy' is?" she asked with a superior air. "That is Elise DeFarge, from Noireau in Paris. She is the primary judge of The Total Noireau Woman contest. I thought everyone knew that by now."

"Of course *we* knew that," Paisley said. "I was just testing to see if *you* knew—isn't that a riot?"

"Hilarious," Michelle sniggered. She turned to Kelly. "By the way, I could not help but notice you talking to that cute cowboy yesterday. He looked like he might be someone important."

"Oh, no," Paisley interrupted. "Him, important? Why, he and his friend are just two fresh college guys—you know the type, all show but no dough. They wanted Kelly and me to go *bowling* with them. Can you imagine? Bowling!" She laughed uproariously.

Michelle narrowed her eyes. "Just college boys, eh?" With a flounce, Michelle left them.

"Whew—what's her problem?" Kelly asked.

"Her pitiful little brain is too small for that big head of hers," Paisley said absently, "and sometimes it rattles around so much she thinks she's come up with an idea."

Kelly let out a peal of laughter. "That's funny."

"Is it?" Paisley's eyebrows rose in surprise. She linked her arm through Kelly's. "Then it's probably the only laugh we'll get out of Michelle Chalfonte. Watch out for her. I've heard she's always trying to steal someone's boyfriend."

"I think you took care of her," Kelly giggled, "but just in case, we could always ask her if she'd like to join our bowling team."

Paisley hooted. "Here we are laughing our heads off, with that Noireau woman sitting ten feet away from us. We must be crazy!"

"You're right." Kelly sobered immediately. "I can't believe we didn't know who she was. That's what we get for going back to our room last night and ordering room service—we missed the gossip. But you know what I think? I think she *was* taking notes on you, Paisley, because she thinks you're going to be the next Miss Noireau."

"You're not serious."

"Of course I am. She was staring right at you." Kelly grabbed Paisley by the elbows in her excitement. "Think of it—you, the next Miss Noireau. Think of the honor, the money, the fame . . ."

"My, my, what would Chad say if he heard his modest little Sugar going on about such ambitions."

"Don't be ridiculous; I'm sure he'd be thrilled if either of us won the contest. And, anyway, don't change the subject. I think you have a good chance of winning the contest and getting the contract."

"Forget it. If Elise DeFarge was staring at anyone, it was you," Paisley insisted. "I'm not even thinking about that contest."

"Why not?" Kelly was genuinely surprised. "Even Loretta said you had a European look, with your pale skin."

"Ha! Don't believe everything you hear. French designers don't go for the dramatic redhead type. They just *love* brunettes. I'm resigned to *not* getting this contract."

"You shouldn't feel that way. Everyone has an equal chance to win."

"Equal chance? What do you think this is, the Girl Scouts? There's no such thing as an 'equal chance' in modeling. Listen, I have a policy—never let yourself care about a job. That's the rule I live by. I know plenty of girls who would fight tooth and nail for a juicy assignment, but face it, there's nothing you can do. Either you have what they want or you don't. It's a cruel business. Denise Cathcart had to quit FLASH! this year because she couldn't take it."

"Denise Cathcart—I remember, a thin, pretty blond. I didn't know she'd quit. But why? She was gorgeous!"

"Gorgeous isn't enough." Paisley shrugged matter-of-factly. "Her kind of looks just weren't in this year. Poor Denise couldn't understand why she wasn't making it big. Everyone had always raved about her looks—you're so beautiful, they'd say, you should go to New York and be a model, you'd be a superstar, you could get into the movies. So she came, and FLASH! took her on, but she just wasn't getting the big jobs. Dramatic, ethnic looks are big right now, not pretty little blonds. So Denise decided she wasn't thin enough. She nearly starved herself to death. Finally she collapsed on a job and Meg told her parents to take her home and fatten her up and let her lead a normal life. She just didn't have what it takes."

"I guess I've been really lucky," Kelly said quietly, "to get into FLASH! and get some great assignments."

"You? You're a phenomenon."

Kelly was thoughtful. "Even if that's true, it's not going to get me everything. Paisley, let's forget all about this name-switching. I mean it. It's going to get us into more trouble than it's worth."

Paisley threw up her hands in exasperation. "Did you know you have a one-track mind? I told you, we can keep Gerard and Chad completely separate from our work. Look, it's done and settled. We won't see them until nine o'clock tonight, and until then, no one around here will hear a word about Sugar and Sunny. Okay?"

Kelly knew when she was licked. "Okay, I guess nothing terrible will happen."

"I'm getting awfully tired of this dressing room," Paisley complained, pulling her dressing gown tightly around her waist.

Kelly had to agree. Waiting their turns at the makeup table seemed to be taking forever. "I know it's because we have our dates later tonight," she said. "And waiting for something always makes the day seem endless." She put a hand over her stomach. "I don't know if I have before-the-big-show butterflies or before-the-big-date butterflies."

"Me, either. I just hope we're not this busy the rest of the week."

"We will be." Kelly sighed.

Paisley glanced at the dressing-room clock. "Three more hours until I see Gerard again."

"You're really stuck on him, aren't you?"

"I seem to be," Paisley admitted. "He was fun to talk to on the phone last night. Things can only get better from here on in. I wonder how I'd feel living in Texas full-time," she mused.

"Now you really are getting carried away."

"You never know—stranger things have happened. The women in my family have always married young."

Kelly rolled her eyes as Rolf, the makeup man, motioned her into a chair before the brightly lit mirror.

"Have you ever used Noireau cosmetics?" he asked her.

"No, never."

"Then you're in for a surprise," he told her knowledgeably. "They can do wonders. Watch how I do this and you'll be able to do it yourself at home."

"I don't wear much makeup at home," Kelly started to explain.

"Oh, she doesn't mean that," Paisley said hastily. "She's always conscious of her appearance, aren't you, Kelly?"

"Not really, I don't bother . . ."

"Sure she does. Just the other day she told me how her ideal is to be attractive all hours of the day. That is the Noireau philosophy, isn't it?" Paisley asked innocently.

"It certainly is," Rolf said.

"Oh—oh, I get it," Kelly muttered. She rolled her eyes and mouthed a thank-you at Paisley. "Yes, it's true. While I'm not very familiar with Noireau's products, I'd certainly like to be, because I agree with the Noireau philosophy." She looked at Paisley. "The Noireau woman is . . . attractive all day long."

"Close enough," Paisley murmured.

"Your skin takes this makeup beautifully," Rolf said as he worked. "Very nice, very nice—see what a difference that makes?"

Kelly looked at her reflection in the mirror. "It *does* do a lot for me," she said sincerely.

"You look fantastic." Paisley grimaced. "I can't wear those vivid colors the way you can, Kelly. I guess I'm stuck with the pale, anemic look."

Rolf laughed and snapped the white towel away from Kelly's neck. "You're next, paleface." He installed Paisley in front of the mirror.

Loretta came by and looked at Kelly. "Rolf, darling, you have done a marvelous job on Kelly Blake," she said, ignoring Paisley completely. "I love what you did with her eyes; they are the brightest things in Houston tonight."

"They are the brightest things in Houston tonight," Paisley mimicked under her breath.

"If Rolf makes you look that spectacular all week . . ." she said to Kelly and paused. "Well, we'll see."

Rolf made a noncommittal sound and continued working on Paisley.

As soon as he was done, Paisley sprang from her chair and grabbed Kelly. "Loretta thinks you're going to be Miss Noireau. I should be jealous, but since I'd already guessed I'll just say congratulations."

Kelly flushed. "Don't start rumors. She didn't actually say anything definite." But she couldn't keep the excitement out of her voice.

Behind her, the other girls were already murmuring, passing the news around the dressing room. "Did you hear—looks like Kelly Blake is it—she's going to be Miss Noireau."

"You hear that, Kelly—they all think that's what Loretta meant."

"Loretta isn't the one who'll make the decision," Kelly pointed out, trying to sound calm and reasonable while her mind raced wildly. *Could it be true—could it be me?*

"Not the final decision," Paisley agreed, "but she gives her opinion, I'm sure."

Overhearing, Rolf shook his head. "Listen to you girls. This is only your second day, but you've already picked a winner. No one's made any decisions yet, believe me."

"But if Loretta does have anything to do with who wins, you'd better watch yourself, Paisley," Kelly said sternly. "You're not exactly subtle, making fun of everything she says."

"I just don't like the old goat," Paisley said stubbornly.

"And why not?"

"I just don't. I don't like her looks."

"That's a terrible reason not to like somebody!" Kelly said. "And if Meg hears about it she'll be furious."

"Meg, schmeg. I have to think about *something* before a show, otherwise I get nervous."

"Then concentrate on the job and leave Loretta alone."

Paisley rolled her eyes. "Oh, all right, I'll try." She raised her fingers to her lips, ready to nibble on her nails, but Rolf smacked her hand.

"None of that—you'll ruin your manicure. Listen to your friend. Relax and think about the show."

"Doesn't anybody around here mind his own business?" Paisley sulked. "I'll bite my nails if I feel like it. They're mine, aren't they?"

"Not tonight they aren't," Rolf threatened. "Shall I get Loretta to watch you?"

"Not that, please," Paisley said dramatically, "anything but that."

"Ignore her," Kelly pleaded. "She really is just nervous."

"She should be nervous," Rolf snapped. "There's a packed house out front, and make no mistake—Houston women are savvy. They know fashion, and they know a good presentation when they see one."

"Stop," Kelly protested, "now you're making *me* nervous."

"Nerves never killed anyone," Rolf said. "Wait a minute, Paisley, I want to tone down your blusher. There. You look fabulous."

"Ugh—I look half dead," Paisley complained. "I hate this flat makeup; it takes all the color out of my face."

"Can't you think of anything positive to say?" Rolf remonstrated.

"Yes, at least you covered my freckles."

As usual, Kelly waited until the last second to shrug off her makeup robe and let the dresser pull a flimsy silk day dress over her head.

"Another modest one," the dresser quipped. "It's okay with me, as long as you don't hold up the line. That's your cue."

She gave Kelly a little push, and Kelly found herself on the other side of the curtains at the beginning of the runway.

It wasn't the first time she'd faced a fashion runway, but nevertheless, the murmur of the audience, the bright bursts of flashbulbs popping, the applause, and the hundreds of pairs of eyes fixed on her gave Kelly a feeling that was becoming part of her now, part of her life. She felt nervous tension, excitement, and exhilaration, all at the same time.

It was the same kind of thrill she used to get from finishing first in a race at a track meet, but now she preferred to get it from modeling. Music blared all around her, and she pranced along the runway in time to the beat, smiling buoyantly at the crowd. The crowd showed its appreciation by applauding loud and long.

"Whew, good reaction," she said breathlessly as she pushed through the curtains and emerged backstage.

"They love Noireau in this town," the dresser told her.

But they also loved me, Kelly thought. Skillfully, the main dresser lifted Kelly's dress off while her assistant slipped Kelly's second costume over her head.

Kelly smoothed her mussed hair and took a deep breath. The music and applause from outside echoed in the backstage area. Over the noise, the commentator's voice rang out.

". . . and for those long days at the office that turn into long nights at a restaurant, Noireau's perfect little black dress. This time in velvet . . ."

"That's you," the dresser exclaimed, giving Kelly a tap that sent her out through the curtains again.

As Kelly traveled the runway this time, aware of the crowd's admiring murmurs, she noticed a well-dressed woman pushing her way to the edge of the raised platform. Elise DeFarge, notebook in hand—she really *was* interested in Kelly!

Kelly tried not to stare, but she could barely suppress an urge to leap the rest of the way. She reminded herself sternly that the black velvet called for a sophisticated stride. A lot of acting was involved in runway modeling, and if you really wanted to be good, you had to express the personality of an outfit through your runway presentation.

She crashed through the backstage curtains exuberantly this time, searching for Paisley.

"Paisley, guess what," she called breathlessly, yanking her arm out of the velvet dress. "DeFarge really seemed to be watching me. She was out by the side of the runway taking notes again."

"What did I tell you? I'm *completely* positive you're going to win this contest. The rest of us might as well go home."

Kelly hugged herself. "I'm having the time of my life out there tonight. I'm going to be so *European* that Elise DeFarge will think she never left Paris."

For once Kelly didn't flinch as the dressers stripped her down to her nude-colored bodysuit and pulled a tightly fitted evening gown over her head.

"Go for it," Paisley encouraged. "If anyone but me is going to win, I'd rather it was you than *some* people I know." She nodded toward Michelle.

Rolf hurried over to apply quick repairs to their mussed hair and makeup. They were ready for the next-to-last number: a procession of Noireau's evening fashions. One after the other, the models would parade down the runway, in a nonstop display of formal gowns, each a different pastel shade than the one before. It was a guaranteed showstopper, and Kelly's only regret was that she was first in line. The last girls always made more of an impact than the first.

That, plus the fact that she envied Paisley's gown, spoiled her pleasure a little. Paisley's pale peach chiffon gown was much nicer than her own pale green dress.

"This pastel color doesn't do a thing for me," she complained. "And it's cut so low I feel like I'm going to fall right out of it."

"You look fabulous," the dresser assured her. "Stop scrunching up your shoulders. For heaven's sake, be proud of that body."

"She's right," Paisley said. "Make the most of what you've got, and show your personality."

Taking her place in line between Kelly and Paisley, Michelle Chalfonte snickered, loud enough for everyone to hear. "She has personality all right—she is the biggest snoot I ever saw. I cannot stand her or her redheaded friend."

All the girls waited to see what would happen next. Kelly bristled. Paisley glowered. Neither of them said a thing.

"Kelly, that's your cue," the dresser said. "You'd better get out there or you'll throw off the timing of the whole number."

With a jolt, Kelly realized the music had started the theme for the procession and the commentator was already describing her gown.

She pushed through the curtains, standing alone momentarily on the runway. Every eye in the audience was focused on her and the picture she made in the lovely pale green dress, her thick brown hair waving down her shoulders.

In a minute, Michelle came through the curtains, followed by Paisley, and then each of the other girls. One behind the other they paraded down one side of the runway and pirouetted at the foot while flashbulbs burst around them; the audience kept up a steady applause, so loud no one could even hear the commentary.

Kelly led the way up the opposite side. Behind her, over the din of applause, she heard Michelle whisper, "This should take Your Highness down a peg or two."

A hair clip dropped onto the runway—right in Kelly's path.

It was a dirty trick. Hairpins and combs were easily jogged loose while models pranced along runways to music. If Kelly were to trip, no one would be able to prove Michelle had dropped the clip on purpose.

Kelly swiftly kicked the hair clip to one side and went on. Michelle muttered something in French that Kelly couldn't catch.

Kelly felt her blood begin to boil, but she could do nothing onstage. She made it through the backstage curtains, then turned to watch the rest of the line.

As Kelly watched, Paisley closed the gap in the line until she was inches from Michelle. Then she carefully brought her foot down on the hem of Michelle's evening gown.

Michelle went to take a step forward. She stumbled awkwardly, tottered for a moment, and threw out her arms to balance herself. There was a gasp from the crowd and then nervous laughter as Michelle found her footing. Meanwhile, Paisley held out her hands toward Michelle, as if she was going to catch her.

"What a clod," she whispered, loudly enough for most of the models nearby to hear.

Michelle blushed a dark shade of red that left blotches scattered over her fair complexion.

Kelly was taking off her gown by the time Paisley and the other girls trooped through the curtains.

"I saw what you did to Michelle," she said to Paisley, as the other girl ran past, her face hidden in her hands. "I know she deserved it, but . . . she's not crying, is she?"

"Oh, she just had a little accident," Paisley gloated.

Kelly shook her head. Happily, she would be one of the last models out for the final number; more evening gowns, but in deep, vibrant shades this time.

"Now this is a dress I like," she exclaimed as a deep sapphire velvet slipped over her head. It was a dramatic gypsy-style gown that rode low on the shoulders, exposing more breast than she usually cared to show, but so flattering and beautiful that for once she didn't care.

Deftly, Rolf dusted her neckline and shoulders with loose powder to take away any shine.

"This dress suits you," he told her. "And you

seem to like it, too. I see you're not slouching anymore."

"I feel too dramatic to slouch," she confessed. "I love it."

Loretta hurried over. "That dress needs a spunky presentation," she warned her.

"I have plenty of spunk—just watch." Kelly tossed her head.

At her cue, Kelly plunged through the curtains. A loud and immediate gasp of audience approval greeted her. She felt drunk on the applause and let herself go wild with it, shrugging the dress off one shoulder, knowing that it was pinned securely to her bodysuit. She played with her hair, tossing it seductively for the photographers lining the runway.

She lifted an arm and swept back her long hair, flipping it completely over her head so it all cascaded down one side of her face. Flashbulbs were popping like crazy, and the applause was deafening. She was creating a sensation and she loved it.

She finished her turns, but the audience wouldn't let her go. At the foot of the runway, she spun wildly. Laughing in exhilaration, she tossed her head again and finally turned for her last walk up the runway. She lifted her head for a farewell smile—and there was Chad, standing deep in the crowd, staring at her with a completely astonished look on his face.

Kelly froze. Next to Chad, Gerard lifted his ten-gallon hat and waved it wildly, grinning from ear to ear. Kelly's eyes met Chad's and he flushed, and suddenly Kelly wasn't a wild and carefree gypsy, but a suburban girl from New Jersey, half-naked on a stage in front of hundreds of strangers. She smiled weakly, sensing the audience's confusion as Chad looked away from her.

Her temper flared. Why should she let Chad, a virtual stranger, spoil her moment in the spotlight? Lifting her head proudly, she looked Chad's way and gave a little curtsy. Gerard waved his hat in response, letting out a rebel yell that echoed over the hall. Kelly laughed. The audience cheered, and she flew toward the curtain for a final bow accompanied by riotous applause.

Backstage she grabbed Paisley. "Guess who's outside. I thought you said they wouldn't get mixed up in our work life."

"They came here?" Paisley peeked around the curtain. "Where are they? Never mind, I see Gerard's hat. This is great—wait till he sees me in this number!" Paisley held out the skirt of her shocking pink gown. Kelly frowned. "What's wrong with you?" Paisley snapped. "I think it's terrific that they came to see us."

"I don't know—I was really hamming it up onstage, and Chad didn't look too pleased about it."

"It's his own fault if he didn't like what he saw. He wasn't supposed to be here at all."

"I know. I guess I'll go change."

"See you in a minute." Paisley waved and stepped to the curtains to wait for her cue.

Six

Without their extravagant clothes and daring makeup, Kelly and Paisley drew no attention from the last few shoppers in the Galleria's plaza; they were simply two teenaged girls hurrying to meet their dates.

Chad was standing with Gerard next to a fountain. Kelly felt, by turns, anxious and annoyed that he might have disapproved of her runway performance. She noticed Chad was wearing a sport coat, and his ten-gallon hat was nowhere in sight. He made a handsome date, and Kelly suddenly hoped he still wanted to go out with her.

"Hi," she said lightly. "Here I am."

Chad raised his eyebrows at the sight of Kelly's matching turquoise shirt and skirt and cuffed denim jacket. "Aren't those clothes pretty plain for you?"

"I don't usually wear an off-the-shoulder designer gown, if that's what you mean," she answered coolly.

"Don't get me wrong," he said hastily, "you looked—uh, awfully attractive in the fashion show. But I have to admit I was a bit thrown. I thought you were a quiet type of girl."

Kelly felt a keen disappointment. "What did you expect me to wear at a designer fashion show—long underwear?"

"Well, now, I see that . . ." Chad cleared his throat. "I'm saying this all wrong." He smiled awkwardly. "What I meant was, I was kind of worried that you'd think I'm not your type."

Relieved, Kelly forgave him instantly. "Oh, Chad, don't worry, that was just my stage act. It's my job to be, well, theatrical."

"You were theatrical all right." Chad seemed relieved, too, almost embarrassed. "The audience loved you."

"Thanks. If it helps any, this is the real me." She gestured at her unassuming outfit.

"You don't have to explain anything," Chad insisted. "But I guess I'm a down-home, straight-dealing kind of guy, and if that doesn't suit you, well, I just thought we should get it out in the open right away."

"Whew," Kelly said with a smile, "that's quite a speech. But don't worry. I'm a down-home, straight-dealing kind of girl myself."

Chad's handsome face relaxed into a grin.

"Good—that's what I thought the first time I saw you."

"Now that that's settled," Gerard boomed, "let's get this show on the road. How 'bout findin' a place for some eatin' and dancin'. Do you gals know how to do the Texas two-step?"

"Not me, but I'm a fast learner," Paisley trilled.

"That's the spirit." Gerard led them to the parking lot, where a late-model Bronco gleamed under a streetlamp.

"I left the Corvette home tonight, seein' as there's four of us to haul around."

"A Corvette, too—my, my." Paisley glanced approvingly at the Bronco. Chad held the door while Kelly got into the backseat.

"It's really nice of you both to take us out tonight," Kelly said as soon as they were all settled, "but I ought to warn you about something." She ignored Paisley's snort of impatience. "It's just that Loretta is in charge of all the models for the time we're here, and we have this sign-in system to make sure we get back at a reasonable hour . . ."

"Shoot," Gerard grumbled, "we haven't even started and already you're tellin' us that we have to stop."

"Don't worry, Gerard," Paisley told him, "I can squeeze in a few extra minutes without Loretta finding out."

Kelly winced. "I'm not trying to be a spoil-sport," she explained, feeling foolish, "it's just that you might as well know now that we have to be back by a reasonable hour."

"Don't worry about it, Sugar," Chad said easily. "After all, if you're as busy all week as you were today, you'll need a good night's sleep. We'll get you back as early as you like."

Kelly smiled at him gratefully. "Thanks for understanding. Some guys think all models lead a pretty fast life, but Pai—Sunny and I aren't like that. Are we, Sunny?"

Paisley glared at her. "We're not children, either."

"Exactly how old are you?" Gerard asked. "The drinking age here is twenty-one. You're of age, I hope?"

"Of course," Paisley said. "I'm twenty-one, and Sugar is . . ."

"I'm sixteen," Kelly said quickly, returning Paisley's dirty look. Kelly wasn't about to add another lie to the lie about her name.

"That doesn't bother me," Chad said. "I don't care much about drinking myself. I have to work early in the morning."

Chad leaned back against the seat, apparently having said all he intended to say for a while. He remained silent as the big car rolled along the highway.

Meanwhile, Gerard kept up a steady conversation with Paisley. "I thought that show you did was real excitin'. I loved watchin' you out there. You do a good job at . . . What do you call it, anyway?"

"Runway work, I guess," Paisley said.

"The way you do runway work, Sunny, I could watch it all night."

"Why, thank you, Gerard. You sure know how

to flatter a girl." Paisley sat a little closer to him on the front seat.

"It's not flattery if it's the truth," Gerard told her admiringly.

According to Gerard, everything Paisley said or did was absolutely wonderful. Kelly thought the way he gushed over her was absolutely sickening. But maybe that was only sour grapes, because Chad was so silent on the seat next to her.

He's a strange kind of boy, Kelly thought. *So serious and quiet about everything*. She realized that she didn't know much about him, but she hesitated to ask any questions. *Oh well, I have the whole evening to solve the mystery of Chad Renfrew. I guess I'll find out all about him soon enough.*

But hours later, after having eaten a huge bowl of the Texas chili that was the specialty of Chudder's Texas Jamboree, and well into her fifth dance with Chad, Kelly still hadn't learned a thing about her mysterious date.

She watched the expression on his handsome face as they danced. Chudder's was crowded (despite the fact that it was five times bigger than any club or restaurant Kelly had ever seen), and from time to time other couples bumped into them. When someone stomped on his toes, Chad always nodded pleasantly and made a light, friendly remark, and Kelly could see that people naturally respected him. He had an easy air of authority about him that made him seem older than he was. Yet at other times, when they were dancing, for example, his eyes lit with a fleeting, childlike pleasure that made him look like a little boy. He was a mystery, all right.

"They don't have places like this in New Jersey," she cried breathlessly as they danced, "where everyone parties together, young people and families and even grandparents. It's great—I love it!"

Chad smiled and swung her around in a wide arc.

"I'd like to see the rest of the place. Do they really have a mechanical bull? I can't believe there's pinball and pool and video games, too. Whoever said everything is bigger in Texas wasn't kidding."

Wordlessly, Chad smiled down at her.

Kelly's temper flared. "Listen, Chad . . . maybe I shouldn't say this, but are you *trying* to act mysterious or something? We haven't had anything resembling a conversation all night, and I'm beginning to feel stupid, talking to myself! At least tell me to shut up if you don't want to listen."

"What?" He gazed at her, looking startled and offended.

"Oh, me and my big mouth," she said, wishing she could kick herself. "Look, I didn't mean to sound so crabby. Maybe you have a reason to be so quiet. Maybe you already have a girlfriend, and you think I'm trying to get involved with you. Really, I'm not. I know it's just one date, so forget I even mentioned it."

"No, no, Sugar," he protested. "You're absolutely right. You'll have to forgive me. It's been so long since I was out with a girl like you . . . I guess I forgot how to do the right things."

"Forgot how . . ." Kelly was perplexed. "I don't understand why you keep saying things like that. You make it sound like you've been locked away for years." Her eyes widened in alarm. "You haven't been in jail, or anything, have you?"

"No—my gosh, no, nothing like that." Chad stopped dancing. "I can't explain, it's . . . Oh, this is no place to talk, anyway."

"Maybe we *should* talk," Kelly said nervously. "About a lot of things."

Chad looked at her and nodded his head. "Come on, let's go outside." Taking her arm, he steered her across the crowded dance floor, past the table where Gerard and Paisley were laughing uproariously at some joke, and out through a rear door. Slowly, they walked away from the building. It was quiet back there, and dark, with only scattered stars and a bright moon to light the path in front of them.

It was a dazzling sight. Kelly felt elated by the wide-open space all around them. She wasn't used to seeing so much land and sky at once. The night was amazingly clear, the air crisp enough that Kelly would have welcomed a friendly arm around her shoulder. She glanced at Chad, but he made no such move.

He didn't talk, either. Finally Kelly cleared her throat.

"Chad, um, I always like to get to know a lot about the people I date . . ."

Chad interrupted. "I know how you feel." He

shook his head as if clearing his thoughts. "But I don't talk about it much. Not to anyone."

"Talk about what?" Kelly was totally confused. "Look, maybe I shouldn't know this secret of yours."

"I have to tell you," Chad insisted. "I want you to know more about me. Look, it isn't a girl, it's nothing like that." He took a deep breath. "It's about my parents."

Kelly frowned in confusion. "Your parents? Do they have a country-club girl all picked out for you, or something?"

"No, it's not like that, it's . . ." Chad bit his lip. "My parents are dead. They were cattle ranchers, and they were riding the range in a helicopter that crashed . . ."

"Oh, Chad, I'm sorry." Kelly wanted to reach out and comfort him, but she kept her distance. It was obviously hard for him to tell her this, and she didn't want to make it any harder.

"I was away at school when it happened. My sophomore year. At first I didn't want to come home to the ranch. I couldn't bear to see it again, with both of them gone. It was so sudden, you know," he said, as if he had to apologize for his feelings.

"I understand," Kelly said softly.

"Anyway, I got over that feeling. Had to— there was a whole legal mess to straighten out. They'd left the ranch to me, and, well, most of the employees quit or started looking for work right after . . . the accident. I can't blame them—who wants a raw college kid for a boss? But a few decided to stay on, and our ranch manager, Hank Clay, well, he's been with the ranch since before I was born. He stayed on, and convinced me to make a go of it."

"It must've been awfully hard on you." Kelly tried to imagine what she would do if anything happened to both her parents. It was unthinkable—she and Tina alone in the world. "It must've taken a lot of courage."

Chad's voice became businesslike again. "I don't know about courage, but it took hard work. I doubled my course load and finished college early. Then I came home to manage the ranch. It's been almost a year now, but textbooks can't teach you everything you need to know. I've still got a lot to learn."

"I'm sure you can do it," Kelly said sincerely. "You seem so—competent, I guess the word is."

"Thanks. I've been working full-time with Hank ever since, without much of a break or even a day off. Skip practically had to drag me into Houston yesterday."

Kelly looked at him with admiration. "You haven't had time for much of a social life, have you?"

He seemed grateful that she understood. "Mostly it's been Hank and me and the ranch. But you were wrong about one thing you said inside. I do want to get involved—more than anything, I want to get involved—with the right girl."

Instinctively, Kelly laid her hand over Chad's. Chad turned his hand over, palm to palm with hers, and a spark of warmth flowed through her. They were both silent, thinking their own thoughts and gazing over the Texas landscape.

The spicy scent of flowers drifted on the night air, and Kelly felt melancholy and suddenly lonely.

"Hey, it must be pretty late," Chad said. He released Kelly's hand and peered at his watch. "We'd better be getting you on home. Come on."

Inside, Gerard and Paisley were cheering a contestant on the mechanical bull.

"We can't go anywhere now, buddy," Gerard said flatly. "I've got twenty dollars ridin' on Jimmy there, and I aim to stay around and collect my winnin's."

Kelly grabbed Paisley's shoulder and yelled over the cheering crowd. "We've got to get back and sign in. Remember, you want to stay on Meg's good side."

"I know, but you heard Gerard, we have to see how the contest goes. You should see this guy Jimmy ride—he's phenomenal!"

"Sunny," Kelly said in a warning tone, "you've got to sign in on time."

"We're having too much fun to leave," Gerard interrupted. "Here—you-all take my keys and go on back. I know people here. Sunny and me will get a ride back with somebody else."

Kelly tried one more time. "But you have to sign in, *Sunny* . . ."

"I will sign in, Sugar," Paisley said impatiently, "and right now I don't care how late."

"Come on, Sugar," Chad said, "I'll get you back on time, anyway. I know Skip, and when he's partying, you can't make him stop until he wants to stop."

"I guess so," Kelly said. "If you think it's safe for them to drive with someone else . . ."

"They'll be fine," he assured her. "Don't worry about that. Besides, this way, I get to drive home alone with you."

She felt a shiver of anticipation when he said that, but Chad was his silent self again in the car. They barely talked all the way back to the hotel. Chad spoke only to point out local landmarks whizzing by as they sped down the highway, and he kept both hands firmly on the wheel. Kelly felt vaguely disappointed.

"Thanks for getting me here on time," she said politely as Chad parked the car. "I'd better go in. Thanks again."

"Hold on. Don't rush off like that." Chad opened her car door for her, then took her firmly by the elbow. "I'll walk you inside. This place is pretty deserted at this time of night."

"But I'm fine on my own," Kelly insisted, imagining an awkward moment in the lobby with Loretta lying in wait, exposing Kelly as a fraud.

But Chad wouldn't take no for an answer. He walked Kelly to the registration desk in the hotel lobby, where the clerk showed them the models' sign-in sheet. Kelly began to sign in next to her own typed name, but at that moment, Chad leaned forward. Quickly she signed in as Paisley Gregg.

"We made the eleven-thirty curfew, anyway," she said, glancing at the hotel clock. "Only three minutes before, but on time nonetheless. Well . . . I suppose you'd better go, Chad. It's pretty late."

"No, I'll wait for an elevator with you. Where are they around here, anyway?"

Kelly heard chattering voices and she stiffened. What if she was discovered now? Just then, Michelle Chalfonte and several other models came into sight.

"These elevators are the fastest," Kelly cried, dragging Chad quickly to the elevator furthest away from the desk.

"Aren't those girl models?"

"Yes, but you wouldn't like that noisy crowd."

Michelle spotted them, and called loud goodbyes to the other models while hurrying toward Kelly. "Hello there, you two," she said breathlessly. "Wait up. I see you changed your minds about bowling."

Chad looked perplexed. "Sugar and I didn't go bowling. Never even thought of it."

"Sugar?" Michelle raised her eyebrows.

"That's right," Kelly said hastily. "Chad won't call me anything else, and he won't let anybody use any other name for me, isn't that right, Chad?" She smiled flirtatiously.

"What a perfectly adorable nickname," Michelle gushed. "I am just plain Michelle." The way she said it, the name Michelle sounded anything but plain. Somehow, Michelle managed to wedge herself between Kelly and the elevator door so Kelly ended up squashed in a corner while Michelle was squeezed close to Chad. "You know, Chad, somehow *Sugar* gave me the impression that you were a champion bowler. You do look like an athlete."

"Thank you kindly for the compliment," Chad said.

"Did you hear that?" Michelle exclaimed. "I

love the way Texans are always so polite." She gazed into Chad's eyes, linking arms with him.

Kelly couldn't believe what was happening. Chad just stood there, smiling politely at Michelle! Kelly turned her head away and punched at the elevator button, praying it would come instantly. She wanted to hide inside it and never come out. But the elevator seemed to take forever.

She wished she could just disappear. She felt thankful to be off in a corner where no one could see her embarrassment. *How can he stand there flirting with her—unless Michelle is his type. Well, if he can't tell a complete phony when he sees one, there's nothing I can do about it!*

The elevator doors slid open, and Chad took Michelle's elbow and helped her inside. Kelly felt sick to her stomach.

She started to follow Michelle, intending to stand in the back corner, but Chad stepped between her and the closing elevator doors so Kelly couldn't go anywhere.

"Aren't you coming?" Michelle exclaimed in surprise.

"We'll catch the next one," Chad answered with a smile as the doors closed in front of Michelle's startled face.

Kelly's mouth dropped open.

"Why do you look so surprised?" Chad laughed softly. "Couldn't you tell I wanted to get rid of her?"

"I—I wasn't sure," Kelly said, ashamed to admit the truth.

Chad took her in his arms and kissed her

gently on the top of her head. For a long moment, he stood there motionless. Kelly held her breath. Pressed lightly against Chad's chest, she was afraid to breathe, afraid to spoil the moment. When he released her, her heart was pounding.

"I'd like to take you out to the Triple C sometime," he said, holding her at arm's length. "Would you like that?"

"The Triple C—is that your ranch? Sure, I'd love to go."

"Good. I'd like you to see where I come from. The Triple C means a lot to me. I—I guess you could say it's my whole life now."

Startled by his intensity, Kelly said lightly, "The Triple C—it sounds like something out of an old western."

"It is," Chad told her proudly. "My great-grandfather made up the name. He was Crawford Renfrew, my great-grandmother was Cassie, and my granddaddy, Crawford, Junior, was their only son. They were the original Triple C's. My daddy was named Crawford the Third to carry on the tradition."

"That's a great story." Kelly was smiling less at the story than at the expression on Chad's face as he told it; it was the first time she'd seen him look completely happy.

"It doesn't end there." Chad chuckled. "My mother was named Caroline. Daddy used to tease that the only reason he married her was to keep the tradition of *C* names in the family, but anyone could tell that wasn't true—he was crazy about her."

"You must miss her."

"Well . . ." Chad's voice softened, "I do miss her an awful lot, and him, too." He looked up and tried to joke. "But look at you, Sugar, you're as pretty as she was and you don't have a *C* name at all. Some traditions are worth breaking, I guess."

"Oh, me, I . . ." She stopped, completely flustered. "You barely know me," she protested lamely. She'd almost blurted the truth: that she wasn't Sugar or Paisley at all, but Kelly—Kelly Blake.

"But I could get to know you better," Chad said. "So, if you're free tomorrow . . ."

"Just during the morning. We have a pretty full schedule after that."

"Mornings are best for me, too. If you can be ready early, I'll pick you up at eight. It'll take an hour to get to the ranch if we miss rush-hour traffic. If we don't, we may never get there! You've never seen a traffic jam till you've seen a Houston traffic jam."

"I'll be ready, I promise. But I'll meet you outside the lobby, by the parking lot. I don't want to waste time meeting you in here." *Or risk bumping into anyone who knows me!*

"I'll be there."

Kelly got on the next elevator.

"Till tomorrow," he said, with an arm on each door to stop them from closing.

"Till tomorrow," she repeated. She felt a strange elation as she said the words.

Chad let the doors slide closed. He'd gone without even trying to kiss her good night. He was certainly different from any boy she'd known before. But then, Chad was more than a boy, he was a responsible young man. *I like that*, Kelly thought, smiling foolishly in the empty elevator. *I think I like that a lot.*

Seven

The overhead light went on and Kelly sat bolt upright, rubbing her eyes.

"Oh, did I wake you?" Paisley called loudly, slamming the door. "Sorry."

Kelly glanced at the bedside clock. "Two o'clock! And you're just getting in?"

"Is it that late? It was a *fabulous* night. Gerard's exactly how I thought he'd be." She sighed dreamily.

"Are you crazy? Two o'clock in the morning? Are you trying to get tossed off this assignment before it's even begun?"

"Now look at yourself, honeychile, gettin' all riled up about nothin'. I sure was surprised to see you'd signed in next to my name—but it makes everything perfect! No one cares what time Kelly

Blake gets in. Why, she's as reliable as a barnyard rooster crowin' at the break of day. Why, she's as steady as a—"

"Paisley! If you're going to make excuses, at least drop that phony Texas accent! I can't stand it."

"I thought I did it pretty well."

"That's not the point, Paisley. The point is that even Kelly Blake can't get away with coming in at two in the morning when she's got to work the next day. You've got to make some effort; you can't just run completely wild." She narrowed her eyes. "What were you and Gerard doing so late, anyway?"

Paisley opened the small refrigerator and reached for the packet of brownies. "Umm, these smell good. They *are* good," she said with a full mouth. "Have some, Kelly, they're delicious."

Kelly ignored her. "You know, you've just met Gerard," she said uneasily. "Don't get too carried away, okay?"

Paisley drew back indignantly. "What I do is my business. Anyway, this is one of those cases where you just click with someone—instantly. This could be the start of something good, something really lasting."

Kelly kept her tone light. "That's great, but I wouldn't count on it yet. I mean, I wouldn't . . . do too much with a guy before I'd gone out with him more than once."

"For goodness' sake, I didn't do anything *drastic*, if that's what you mean. Not yet, anyway. But you know how it is, when you completely lose your head over a boy."

Kelly fidgeted. "Not exactly. I'm not sure I ever lost my head."

"You would over Gerard. I don't think I've ever met anyone like him before."

Paisley turned on her bedside lamp and switched off the overhead light. She continued talking as she threw off her dress and dug her pajamas out of a bureau drawer. "I love everything Texan," she exclaimed. "The accents, the food, the dancing. I haven't danced that much in ages! Chad's pretty good, too, I noticed. Lots of girls were watching him tonight, Kel. You'd better be careful or someone's going to steal him away from you."

Kelly felt a ripple of fear. "I hope not."

Paisley gave her a knowing look. "And you still don't think Chad is special?"

"I just met him," Kelly protested. "But were people really watching us? He is a good dancer, no matter what he says about being out of practice. And, Paisley, you don't know—both his parents died in an accident, and Chad has been running their ranch on his own ever since! Isn't that remarkable? He's very mature . . . but so sad, too. I think it's so cruel that he's all alone in the world. You know, when he smiles, he has the tiniest little dimple in his right cheek, and his eyes actually light up. He's probably the best-looking boy I've ever known. Did you notice the way his hair sort of waves over his forehead? He must comb it straight, because it was lying flat at first, but after he was dancing, it curled right up."

"Hold it—you're talking my ear off." Paisley

yawned, climbing into her double bed. "Boy, I thought I had it for Gerard."

"It's not like I'm falling in love or anything," Kelly protested. "It's just that he's interesting and seems to like me. He's taking me to see his ranch in the morning. I can hardly wait. Do you think I could borrow that little Stetson hat you brought along? . . . Paisley, are you listening?"

Paisley had fallen asleep, the brownies spilled in a pile on her bed. Feeling slightly insulted, Kelly got up and moved the brownies onto the night table. Then she turned off Paisley's lamp, got back into bed, and punched up her pillows. But she couldn't sleep; images of Chad were whirling through her head.

"Am I falling for a Texas boy?" she wondered out loud.

She did sleep, finally, and when Chad picked her up at eight on the dot, she felt energized and renewed. She'd dressed especially for a morning on a ranch: jeans, cowboy boots, western-style jacket, and Paisley's Stetson hat.

"You look fresh as a morning breeze," Chad told her as he unlocked the door of the red Ford pickup he was driving. He was dressed in clean, pressed denims, and looking every inch the rancher.

"Get a good night's sleep?" he asked as he helped her into the truck.

"Fabulous. But I couldn't wait to get started today."

"You won't be sorry. The ranch is at its best on

a pretty morning like this." He pulled smoothly out of the parking lot.

"You sound like you've been up for hours."

"I have—since five o'clock."

"Five o'clock!" Kelly exclaimed. "But you hardly got any sleep yourself, then. I kept you out too late last night. I never dreamed you got up so early."

Chad beamed at her. "Last night was special in more ways than one. I was twenty-one years old yesterday."

"Your birthday! And you didn't say anything?" Kelly was astounded. "You should have told me. We could have had a real celebration."

"It *was* a real celebration." Chad put his hand on top of Kelly's.

She glanced down. "You're making me blush." She laughed nervously. "But really, Chad, I wish you'd told me."

"I haven't felt much like celebrating lately," he said, and Kelly felt a pang of guilt for forgetting about his parents' deaths. "Anyway, if I'd done anymore partying last night, I wouldn't be able to manage a ranch full of animals today."

Kelly shook her head. "You really are the responsible type, aren't you?"

Chad squeezed her hand. "Sure am. I hope that's all right with you."

"Of course it is. I wouldn't like someone irresponsible."

"Good. Now let's hope you like the Triple C the way it is, too."

They drove in a pleasant silence, enjoying the fresh, clean air outside the city. Finally, Chad pointed and said, "Here it is. The Triple C land starts right at that fence, where those mesquite shrubs are."

"It's—so open," Kelly marveled, staring at a low, grassy plain with only an occasional windmill turning lazily in the breeze. "I thought we'd see barns and silos and bunkhouses." Around them were miles of open country, dotted with cactus and hackberry trees and aloe plants. "And cattle," she added, "and people."

Chad was amused. "The buildings are closer to the main house, where I live. The people are there, too, don't worry. The cattle have all been rounded up. It's time to sell them, not graze them."

Finally, they came to a row of cottonwoods framing the ranch's main gate.

"And all this land is yours?" Kelly turned in her seat. It seemed so vast.

"I've got several thousand head on the land, and you need twenty to forty acres per cow for grazing. Did you think the wide open spaces out here were a myth?"

"I never really thought about it."

"We don't know much about each other's way of life, do we? Come on, city girl." He grinned tolerantly. "I'll give you the grand tour."

As promised, barns and silos and bunkhouses soon appeared. Chad gave her a brief rundown of modern ranching methods, explaining how machines had replaced cowboys in doing some of the work. "This is the calf cradle," he said, pointing to a metal contraption at the bottom of a long ramp. "A calf comes down the chute, and is put into the cradle. The cradle flips the calf on its side and holds it for branding, dehorning, castration, and inoculation." The cradle was covered with dirt and dried blood.

Kelly shuddered and turned quickly away, trying to seem mature. Castration—was he kidding? "I guess you take those things for granted on a ranch."

"Nobody said it was pretty work. I guess it was more romantic in the old days, but there aren't many young hands who know how to rope and tie a calf from the saddle."

"Like in a rodeo?" Kelly asked. "Where they throw the calf and tie its feet together real fast?"

"That's it. Originally, rodeos were contests to see who was the best at routine ranch work."

"Well, modeling still has contests like that— like the Miss Noireau contest this week. If you win, you get an exclusive contract."

"A pretty girl like you shouldn't have to worry about anything but being pretty."

Kelly smiled tolerantly. "I like working hard at my job too."

"I'll bet you work hard no matter what you do." He led her into the main barn. Hundreds of cattle were at their feed. "They've finished with grazing on pasture. Now their only task is to fatten up for market."

"There are so many!"

"And they keep me busy."

"Maybe it's not exactly like the old days," Kelly said dreamily, "but at least you still work hard in the fresh air, riding the range, getting that good tired feeling you have after really exerting yourself."

"Hold on." Chad laughed. "It can be like that, sometimes. But mostly it's chasing after a dumb cow for hours in a beat-up old truck. And bumping over this ground in a truck is no joyride. That's why we use the helicopter so often."

Kelly quickly changed the subject. "How many employees do you have?"

Chad answered absently, then looked away. She let him think his own thoughts for a while as she gazed around the Triple C. There was so much to take in: the way the air smelled, blowing clean and fresh from the pastures and mingling with the gamey animal smell from the barn; the weathered outbuildings; and off in the distance, the main house, surrounded by rows of flowers and shaded by tall elms.

"What are you thinking?" she finally asked Chad. "You're a million miles away."

He shook his head.

"I'll tell you what *I'm* thinking," she said lightly. "I'm thinking how much I like it here. It feels . . . comfortable somehow, like a real home."

He looked at her gratefully. "I feel that way about it, too. Always have. I thought I might do something else with my life for a while, but then . . . Now I know I'm home for good. And I like that." He took her hand.

"What's in that barn, over there?" She pointed.

"The stables. Want to see them?"

"You do have horses!" Kelly exclaimed as he

led the way. "I was beginning to think horses were too old-fashioned for you."

"Sometimes it's the best way of checking the herd, even nowadays. That's Ruby and Challenger, and this one here is Brutus. Isn't he a beauty?"

"He sure is." Kelly reached up and patted the white star on the horse's nose. "We have time for a ride," she said impulsively. "You could ride Brutus, and I'll ride Ruby. You can show me the Triple C from the saddle, the way it ought to be seen."

"Hold on there, Sugar. I don't want you riding any of these horses. They're used to rough handling and they're a bit rough themselves."

"I'm not the world's best rider," Kelly admitted, "but I've had enough practice to handle a short ride. We don't have to race them or anything."

"It's not a good idea," Chad said firmly. "I wouldn't want you to fall and hurt yourself."

"I wouldn't fall," she scoffed. "Ruby looks too gentle to hurt a fly! Besides, you'll be right there to see that nothing happens."

"You never know what might happen," Chad said stubbornly.

"You're protecting me for no reason," she cried, unable to squelch her annoyance.

"It's not a good idea. Even my mother never rode."

"Really?" Kelly asked.

"She hated horses and the helicopter, too. She only went with my father that day to humor him. She hardly ever went outdoors. Her skin was so fair, she liked to keep out of the sun. But everyone loved her just the way she was," Chad said. "Come on, let's get up to the house."

Kelly tried not to show her astonishment. She had imagined Caroline Renfrew suntanned and fit, riding the range with her husband and the trailhands. Her fantasy obviously needed some heavy revising.

"You're upset about the horses, aren't you?" Chad watched her closely as he helped her back into the truck. "I just don't want anything to happen to you."

She hesitated. "I understand," she finally said, keeping her tone light. "I'm not that good a rider, anyway." She covered his hand on the steering wheel.

Chad glanced at her sideways and smiled. "There's the house. I'll leave the car by the porch and we'll go in through the front door so you can get the full effect."

Up close, the house was bigger than it had seemed, with wings added on each side. The flower gardens had been Caroline's touch, Chad told her. There were more flowers in tubs on the wraparound porch.

"Despite everything you've said about modern ranching," Kelly joked, "I can just picture a crowd of cowboys hitching their mounts to the porch rails. Cars don't seem to belong at the Triple C."

"That's the spirit of the place," Chad agreed.

He pushed open the wide front door, motioning Kelly inside.

She entered the hallway, and gasped. "It's—it's beautiful!"

Ahead of her was a wide, curving stairway. Wood-trimmed archways off the hall led to other rooms. At the back was a huge paned window, sparkling clean, through which she could see a small back patio.

Everywhere was dark polished wood, shining brass trim, and on the floor, thick, darkly colored rugs. Beneath the chandelier, on a gleaming mahogany sideboard, stood an enormous Chinese vase filled with fresh-cut flowers.

"It's so elegant!" she exclaimed.

"You mean you expected socks on the floor and cobwebs hanging from the ceiling?" Chad chuckled. "Maybe there would be if I were on my own. Luckily, I have help."

He pulled a heavy cord by the front door. "Servants' bell," he explained.

Kelly hadn't expected servants, even though she knew Chad couldn't manage a house and ranch alone, and he had said he had a staff, of course. Still . . .

A woman appeared, wiping her hands on a crisp apron. She had dark hair and bright dark eyes.

Chad addressed her in a familiar tone of voice that nevertheless had an air of unquestioned authority to it. "Maria, my friend and I would like a breakfast tray in the library, please."

Maria nodded politely and glanced at Kelly with undisguised interest. The twinkle in her eyes made it clear that she was delighted with Chad's guest. "I'll bring you something nice," she said in a soft voice, with a trace of Spanish accent.

Kelly smiled at her before she left, then turned to Chad. "I thought a servant would be stiff and formal. Maria's not like that at all. She makes me feel comfortable."

"Maria's been part of the ranch for twenty-five years," Chad told her. "Longer than I have. Her husband and two of their sons also work at the Triple C. They're some of the employees who stayed on. I really value them."

Chad quickly led Kelly through the downstairs rooms. There was a formal living room, an informal living room, and two kitchens. One was huge and old—the original kitchen, Chad told her, used mainly to feed extra hands during roundup. The rest of the time, the smaller, modern kitchen was used. Both kitchens connected to a formal dining room with massive wood furniture and a chandelier that matched the one in the hall.

"My mother liked the family to eat in the dining room," Chad explained. "She said it made things more civilized."

"I'll bet it did." Kelly paused to admire the elegant flowered fabrics, the striped silk wall covering, the polished silver—a tea service, candlesticks, pitchers—that gleamed on serving trays, on the generous sideboard, in the handsome breakfront.

"It's so beautiful. Did your mother do all the

decorating herself? It has such a distinctive style."

Chad looked pleased. "She had help from some Houston decorators, but it has her touch. Everyone says it's the prettiest ranchhouse around."

"It's perfect," Kelly said honestly. "Anyone would be proud to own it. You must entertain here a lot. I guess your business requires it."

"I hardly entertain at all anymore," Chad said slowly, "but Maria keeps the place ready, just in case. It feels"—he hesitated—"a little empty to her. She'd like nothing better than to have big dinner parties here again."

Kelly felt that Chad was hinting that the ranch needed a woman's touch, and she didn't know what to say. It was thrilling to imagine herself presiding over dinners in that beautiful dining room. But of course, she'd just met Chad; the idea of marrying him was absurd. She was only sixteen, after all. *Although,* she thought, *my career does make me feel older than that sometimes.* . . . She shook her head to clear the ridiculous notions away. Chad didn't even know her real name!

Eight

They entered the library, a handsome room, furnished with comfortable leather couches. Green velvet drapes hung at the French windows, and the rich dark tones were echoed in the mahogany bookshelves and the large, sturdy desk. A brass pen and pencil set and a brass clock and paperweight gleamed in the light that filtered through sheer curtains.

Kelly spied a tray set on a low coffee table in front of one of the couches. She sat in front of it, examining with pleasure the brightly painted crockery and hefty silver. There were pots of coffee and tea, sliced cake, a basket filled with muffins and rolls, tubs of butter and jam, a plate of sliced fresh fruit, and a pitcher of heavy cream.

"It looks delicious."

"Help yourself." Chad sat beside her.

Kelly felt herself assume the role of well-bred hostess. "What would you like, Chad?" She held up a painted cup, waiting to serve him first.

"Coffee, cream, no sugar, and some of that cinnamon cake with butter."

Lifting the coffeepot, Kelly poured a precise amount of coffee, leaving enough room for the cream. She added the cream and handed the cup to Chad. Their eyes met. She saw approval in his expression. Smiling, she spread a dab of butter on a slice of cake and placed it on a small plate. She shook out a linen napkin and handed it all to Chad.

"Thank you, my dear," Chad teased in an unnaturally formal voice.

Kelly relaxed in the soft glow of Chad's approval. After helping herself, she noticed that Chad waited until she had begun eating before sipping his own coffee.

"What nice manners you have, my dear," she teased back, but she meant it. He did have beautiful manners. She wondered if that was his mother's doing, too.

"Oh, what's that?" She'd spotted a framed photograph standing inconspicuously on a bookshelf. "Do you mind if I look?" Aware that Chad was watching her, she lifted the picture and inspected it carefully. As she had suspected, it was a picture of Chad's parents.

Chad looked exactly like his father, dark and dramatic. "I see where you got your dark eyes," she said lightly. She paused before studying his mother.

Chad's mother had been delicately pretty, with wide-set blue eyes and red hair—a clear auburn shade, lit from behind in the photo so that it became a glowing halo around her striking face.

Chad came up behind Kelly, placing a hand on her shoulder, and she half-twisted to steal a look at his face. He looked tense and unhappy.

"I wish—I wish I could say something—to fill the empty places for you," she stuttered. "But . . . nothing can take away your memory of them; you'll always have that." She felt hopelessly inadequate.

"Thank you," he whispered. "That was the perfect thing to say—it was what I wanted to hear." Gently, he lifted her hair from her shoulders. "You see, you understand me. You know what I need. I know you're young, but you're not too young for that."

He leaned close, and she closed her eyes, anticipating his kiss. But a sharp knock intruded. Kelly jumped. She took a step backward, flushing and embarrassed. A loud, rasping cough echoed into the room.

"Excuse me," a voice said.

Holding out a hand, Chad smiled broadly. "Hank—come in, buddy, there's someone here I want you to meet."

Hank Clay was the ranch manager Chad had told Kelly about. He was older than Kelly had expected, with the kind of leathery, weather-beaten face only an outdoorsman had. Kelly wondered if Chad would look like that someday. Instinctively, she liked Hank; he seemed the type of loyal, hardworking man anyone would like.

She held out her hand. Hank whipped off his beat-up old hat and wiped his hand on his dusty jeans before stepping forward to shake it. On his face was a delighted grin that seemed filled with expectation. Kelly found herself smiling back, but quizzically.

"Well, Sugar, welcome to the Triple C," Hank said. By now the name felt so familiar that Kelly barely noticed his use of it.

"Thank you, Hank." She caught herself giving a little curtsy. "Now where did that come from," she exclaimed, surprised at herself. "I must be growing Texas manners or something. It must be in the air."

Hank laughed heartily, his eyes looking so kindly at her that she felt she'd just made the cleverest remark in the world. She was pleased and flattered, but she was also a little relieved when Chad took the attention away from her.

"What is it, Hank?" he asked. "Anything wrong?"

"That rotten agent Peterson is over in the main barn, picking over the feeders. Says our asking price is too high—only wants to take about two-thirds of the herd we set aside for him."

"Two-thirds!" Chad spoke swiftly and with self-assurance. "Tell him it's all or nothing. That's the deal we agreed on and I won't make any changes now. Tell him if he doesn't like it, he can go somewhere else. I'll get another buyer in here before the day is over."

"Yessir, Mr. Renfrew." Hank's admiration was genuine, but his calling Chad "Mister Renfrew" took Kelly by surprise. "You talk business like a college man, all right. I'll tell that old coot what you said, word for word, and if he don't like it he can take his miserable cheapskate offer and see if he can find a better calf crop somewhere else."

Kelly felt dazed. "What are you talking about? Feeders and calf crops . . ."

Chad looked surprised. "Oh, you want details. Okay, I'll try to explain. See, every fall, we take the spring calves and wean them and take them off pasture and put them onto feeds."

"Haven't they been fed?"

Hank and Chad chuckled. "Sure," Chad said, "they've grazed on pasture land all spring and summer, but now they need heavy feed—hay, grain, things to make them grow. When they're full size, they need to be fattened up for market. We keep some here and fatten them ourselves, but we sell the rest to fattening specialists. Those calves are called feeders. Fall is our busiest time for selling feeders."

"I've never heard of anything like it," Kelly exclaimed. "You mean you breed and raise cows for the sole purpose of fattening them up."

"That's about it. The feeders are sold to fatteners for finishing. The finished cattle are sold to slaughterhouses or to meatpackers."

"Like Gerard's family," she said.

"Like the Offenbachers. You've got it. The finished cattle are graded by quality, and the meatpackers—"

"The meatpackers slice 'em, pack 'em, ship 'em, and sell 'em," she finished. "I heard Gerard say that."

"You've got a head for business," Hank said admiringly.

"Not really," Kelly admitted. "Actually, it seems—inhumane. I mean, you breed the poor things, you make them get born. Then you stuff them until they're fat, and then you sell them to be carved into someone's steak dinner. It seems kind of cruel."

"It's no different from raising chickens or pigs for slaughter."

"I know, but . . . It almost makes me want to be a vegetarian."

"What did you think a cattle ranch was for?" Chad was completely tickled and Hank chortled to himself. "Did you think we knew each cow by name and kept them as household pets? Where would the profit be in that?"

"I don't know," Kelly said, feeling foolish.

"Now don't you go apologizing, Sugar," Hank said. "Your heart's in the right place. Years ago, there were ranchers and cowboys who knew their herds by sight, if not by name. Why, an old-time cowboy had a feel for the animals and a feel for the land. He could tell when a well was about to run dry just by laying an ear to the ground. There used to be pride in the work, and a man was more than a—a cog in some infernal conglomerate!"

"You've touched Hank's sore spot," Chad said.

"But he's right," Kelly said impulsively. "I like the idea of men out riding the range on horseback instead of trucks, and treating the cows as living creatures, not . . ."

"Not numbers in a book," Hank finished hotly.

"You're right, and if things were done the way they were in the old days, there wouldn't have been no blasted helicopters to crash and no one to be killed."

Chad turned pale, and there was a strained silence.

"I'm sorry, Mr. Renfrew," Hank muttered, ducking his head. "I guess I got carried away."

For a moment Chad didn't speak at all. Kelly had no idea what he was thinking, but her heart ached for him. It seemed there was no way to escape reminders of his parents' death on the ranch.

"That's all right, Hank," Chad said quietly. "Listen, why don't I go tell Peterson my terms. I'll just be a minute. Sugar, you wait right here."

Left alone with Hank, Kelly felt at a loss for words. When the silence threatened to go on forever, she cleared her throat. "I, uh, I guess you must be very busy at this time of year," she said politely.

Hank frowned, ignoring her feeble attempt at conversation. "The way I see it is this," he suddenly announced. "That boy needs to be married and settled down. That will keep him here on the ranch. Otherwise, a smart boy like that is bound to lose interest and get himself a city job. Maybe just to get away from his memories."

"I guess that's possible," Kelly said, startled by Hank's vehemence.

"Get him married and settled," Hank continued, "and then me, and Maria and her family, and the other old-timers won't be out of a job, out of a place where we belong. You may think it's selfish of me to go on like this, but it's realistic, Sugar, and you can't blame me for that. Got to be realistic nowadays."

"I suppose you do, Hank."

"Who would hire an old codger like me? Where would I find to go? Anyway," he went on without waiting for an answer, "never thought he'd find himself the right gal to settle down with, but things are looking up now." Hank glanced at Kelly and smiled to himself, backing out the door.

Kelly stared after him, startled by his obvious plans for her, but not really displeased. She couldn't help fantasizing a little herself, imagining she was the perfect blend of realist and dreamer for the Triple C. *But that's silly*, she told herself. *It's just that everyone, from Chad to Maria to Hank, wants Chad to settle down with somebody. That doesn't mean it has to be with me!*

Chad soon returned. "Well, I guess it's time to get you back to the hotel," he said regretfully. "I liked having you around, even if it was just for a short time."

"I liked being here," Kelly said sincerely.

The drive back was uneventful, but Kelly enjoyed the quiet pleasure of sitting next to Chad.

At last he pulled up at the hotel entrance. "I won't have much time to get away in the next few days. All the cattle agents will be coming around. Things didn't work out with Peterson after all—things never go the way you plan. But I'll make time—if I have to—to see you. And I'll call you this evening, for sure."

As she walked through the hotel doors, Kelly felt both smugly satisfied with herself and vaguely bothered. She'd insisted again that it was a waste of time for Chad to come inside with her, and she felt sneaky about it.

But it isn't a big deal. As soon as this assignment is over and Paisley is safely home, why, Chad and I will have a big laugh at Paisley's expense. When it's over . . . I'm really planning on seeing Chad after this assignment ends! Maybe Hank Clay isn't the only one making plans for me.

Franklyn, New Jersey, seemed a universe away. With a start, she realized that she hadn't thought about Eric once. *Well, why should I*, she thought, with a toss of her head. There wasn't anything to think about. She found Paisley backstage, wandering aimlessly behind the curtains as she waited for the midmorning events to begin.

"Hi. I see I made it back in time for the big beauty make-overs," Kelly said pleasantly.

"What's wrong with you?"

Kelly stared at her. "What do you mean what's wrong? All I said was hello."

"It was the way you said it, in your phony Miss America voice." Paisley mimicked her. "Hi everybody, I'm your constantly cheerful and optimistic beauty contestant. Yuck." Paisley grimaced. "It makes me sick when you act like that."

"Okay, okay," Kelly grumbled. "Forget it.

What are we supposed to do for this demonstration?"

"We wait until we're called, that's what. They have these gigantic video screens set up out there, and they do a big before-and-after show for the audience. You know, here's our model looking like something the cat dragged in, but after carefully applying Noireau cosmetics she will become a raving beauty."

Kelly smiled despite herself. "A make-over is how I got discovered by Meg. And you shouldn't make fun of this—Loretta or DeFarge might hear you."

"Who cares if they do? They know this whole make-over is a farce. They take some young model with a gorgeous complexion and put make-up on her, and naturally she looks beautiful. The pitiful thing is that every fat, wrinkled, middle-aged lady in the audience thinks she'll look the same way. Personally, I think the public should be protected from scams like this."

Kelly pursed her lips. "Obviously, you didn't get enough sleep last night and now you're taking it out on Noireau and the rest of the world."

"All right, you diagnosed me, Dr. Kelly. Now, what happened with you? Where were you this morning, anyway?"

"I told you last night—when you woke me up. Chad took me to his ranch this morning."

Paisley whistled. "What was it like? Tell me all about it."

"It was wonderful. It was impressive and beautiful—the biggest place I've ever seen. I mean, acres and acres of land. Did you know one cow needs twenty to forty acres of pasture land? No wonder Texans think big."

"Don't tell me about cows, tell me about Chad. What did he say, how did he act?"

"He acted fine," Kelly said. "He said he loved having me there and wished I could stay longer. And I met his ranch manager, Hank Clay—what a character! He was great, straight out of a Hollywood movie. I really liked him."

Paisley narrowed her eyes knowingly. "Come on, Sugar, spill your guts. Those big eyes of yours are hiding something."

Kelly let out a sigh. "I don't know, it's not a big thing, in fact it's not even a *bad* thing, it's just, well, Chad and Hank and everyone kept gushing over me, about how wonderful it is Chad found me and how much I fit in at the Triple C . . ." She hesitated.

"That's fantastic," Paisley prodded. "So what's wrong?"

"It's just—I get this feeling that it's not really me they're talking about. It's like, I look okay and I seem nice so automatically I'm wonderful and I belong there."

Paisley shook her head as if to unclog her ears. "I don't get it. What's wrong with that? They like you."

"But I'm not sure it's *me* they like. Chad and I are just starting to get to know one another. How can he be so sure about me?" Talking to Paisley now, miles away from the Triple C, Chad's intensity and Hank Clay's hints about marriage suddenly seemed ridiculous.

"That's the screwiest thing I ever heard."

Paisley put her hands on her hips. "Any other girl would be in seventh heaven if a cute, rich guy like Chad felt that way about her, but not our Sugar. She has to second-guess everything."

"Stop calling me Sugar," Kelly complained. "I don't mind when Chad does it, but it's not my name."

"Talk about crabby—I happen to like the name Sugar. It's real cute, and it suits you."

"It doesn't suit me," Kelly said huffily. "Oh, why doesn't everyone just—just leave me alone and let me be myself for a change!" She pushed Paisley aside and stormed off to the dressing room.

Her mouth open in astonishment, Paisley followed. Kelly had found Loretta, who instructed her to put on a plain makeup gown over her street clothes.

"After your makeup is done," Loretta said, "you'll come back here and change into a Noireau day dress. Then all the girls will do a brief runway parade, dressed and made up. After that, our makeup artists will choose ladies from the audience and do make-overs on them."

"Do we have to stick around for that?"

"Certainly," Loretta said. "The whole idea is for the shoppers to see you and the other girls and want to look like you, with Noireau cosmetics and Noireau fashions."

"Certainly," Paisley mimicked. "The whole idea is for them to spend a pile of money."

"Miss Gregg"—Loretta frowned—"I've had about enough of your rudeness. If you cannot be civil to anyone, I suggest you learn to keep your mouth shut. It does not take any more effort to be polite than it does to be rude. You might think about that."

Loretta turned her back on them and went to help some other models.

"Oh, big deal," Paisley grumbled, but her pale complexion flushed a shade darker than usual. "Who cares what the old battle-ax says."

"You should," Kelly snapped. "You really are a pain sometimes, Paisley."

"Thank you, Miss Perfect."

"I'm not perfect. I just know when to keep my mouth shut."

"I know, and you know how to be a professional." Paisley stifled a huge yawn. "Well, I can't help it if losing sleep makes me cranky. I guess I'll be smart like you and keep my thoughts to myself the rest of this morning."

"I'm not so smart and I'm not so professional and I'm not so perfect," Kelly exploded. "And I'm not some timid little hothouse flower that has to be protected all the time, and I won't break if I fall down!"

Paisley drew back. "Well, don't shout at *me* about it."

"Oh, it's not you," Kelly admitted. "I don't know what it is. Maybe I should be alone today."

"Fat chance. It's your turn for a Noireau beauty make-over. I'll see you later."

Nine

Kelly took a deep breath, put a cheerful smile on her face, and strutted onto the stage. Somehow, she was more nervous about being made over in front of people than she was about doing a live runway show or a photography session. Maybe it was because she didn't know exactly what was expected of her. In a photo session the photographer told her what do do; on the runway, the numbers were all coordinated. She hadn't been comfortable at her first make-over, either, at the local shopping mall at home. She was lucky Meg Dorian had seen her potential in spite of that.

Rolf smiled encouragingly as Kelly seated herself at the makeup table. In front of her were an ordinary mirror—and a video camera.

"Don't look at the camera," he said quietly,

"just look in the mirror and pretend the camera isn't there.

"And here's Kelly Blake," he said loudly, introducing her to the audience. "This morning, Kelly is wearing only mascara—of course, a young woman like Kelly looks wonderful without makeup, and for any woman, it's a good idea to let your skin breathe, free of cosmetics, from time to time." He turned Kelly's face toward the mirror.

"Nevertheless, I'm going to dab on some cleanser . . ." He wiped Kelly's face gently. "There—to rid the skin of any impurities. That's a must for all ages."

In the mirror, Kelly suddenly spotted Elise DeFarge in the audience behind her. She sat up straighter in her chair.

"Now, I'm going to tone her skin with freshener," Rolf recited.

"Oh—that's cold," Kelly exclaimed.

Rolf looked at her strangely. "Yes . . . it is chilled. That helps to close the pores. We moisturize . . ." He dabbed lotion onto Kelly's skin. ". . . and now we're going to apply foundation, but only where Kelly needs it to even her skin tone. It isn't necessary to cover the entire face and neck—perhaps only for the most formal occasions."

As Rolf leaned forward with a cosmetic sponge, Kelly flung her hair behind one shoulder and lifted her chin high, angling her head toward the camera. From the corner of her eye, she could see herself in the video screen, magnified larger than life. She looked good, very good!

Opening her eyes wide, she raised her eyebrows as Rolf explained the double row of eyeliner he was using for a special effect. "Oh, it's beautiful," she said, batting her lashes.

"Hold still," Rolf whispered, "I'm afraid I'll poke your eye out."

Kelly held still, but the instant he was finished, she turned to the camera and posed as if for a magazine cover, turning her head this way and that, showing a delighted expression from every angle.

Taking her chin in his hand, Rolf firmly turned her face toward the mirror. "Stay there," he commanded in a whisper. "I've got to finish up quickly."

Kelly obeyed, but at the end of each step—eye shadow, more mascara, blusher, and a final dusting of translucent powder—she made sure to make a theatrical gesture.

"Uh, thank you, Kelly," Rolf said as Kelly ducked her head as if bowing to the audience. Quickly, he ushered her off the stage. Kelly flashed one last blinding smile before ducking behind the curtains, pretending not to see Elise DeFarge scribbling madly in her notebook.

"Hey, great job!" Paisley gushed. "You made everyone else look like dead fish. Compared to you, none of these girls knows a *thing* about showmanship. It's pitiful."

Michelle Chalfonte passed by, as haughty as ever. "What were you doing out there, Kelly? Trying to win the Bozo-the-Clown award? I never saw so much mugging in my life."

"Well, I . . ."

"She looked fantastic," Paisley said hotly. "Not a frozen lump like the other girls."

"The other girls had dignity," Michelle said frostily, sweeping out onto the stage.

"Maybe I did overdo it," Kelly said uneasily. "Loretta said to be natural. Maybe I was acting too much."

Paisley snorted. "There you go, wimping out. For a successful model, you don't have much faith in yourself."

"Sometimes I don't," Kelly admitted.

Paisley pushed aside the stage curtains and peered at Michelle. Suddenly she started gesturing wildly to Kelly. "Come here! Take a look at this!" she crowed.

Kelly looked through the parted curtains and stared. Onstage, Michelle was imitating everything Kelly had just done, only more so; tossing her head, flirting with Rolf, mugging at the makeup mirror. Kelly thought it looked fine when she watched Michelle herself, but when she watched the giant video screen, she squirmed in discomfort.

"Did I look so—exaggerated?"

"Don't be ridiculous, you looked fine," Paisley told her.

"I don't know . . ." She knew that television actors toned down their movements to avoid appearing too theatrical.

"You *want* to be larger than life," Paisley said. "They don't want a Miss Noireau who's *ordinary*. Anyway, imitation is the sincerest form of flattery, and Michelle is too smart to imitate anything bad."

"That's true. She wouldn't do it unless she thought it would impress DeFarge."

"Exactly. Quit worrying. You did a better job than Michelle, and besides, you were the first. Everyone can tell she's copying you."

"I hope so . . . I hope they remember that I was the original one."

In their room after the makeup demonstration, Kelly called home and chatted with her mother for fifteen minutes. Then she and Paisley devoured a hearty lunch from room service.

"I'm starved," Kelly declared. "Who would think that putting on makeup would make anyone so hungry?"

"It wasn't the makeup demonstration— although the way those women pawed over us when we went out on the floor afterward was exhausting. It was your morning at the ranch."

"The ranch . . ." Kelly felt a pang of longing. "I wish . . . I wish I could be with Chad for the rest of my time here. I mean, this assignment is exciting, but if I could somehow be with Chad, too . . ."

"I know exactly how you feel." Wiping her hands and shoving her tray aside, Paisley began pulling on a fresh pair of jeans and an oversized shirt. She flung a bright paisley shawl, her trademark, over one shoulder. "How do I look?"

"You look great, as usual. But why are you dressing when we'll just have to strip downstairs? You'll be wearing a plain robe all afternoon, between costume changes."

"No, I won't be wearing any plain robe."

"I don't get it." Kelly pushed her own tray aside. "You have to wear a robe between changes."

"But I'm not making any costume changes," Paisley told her patiently, "because I'm not going to do any modeling."

"What are you talking about? We have forty minutes to rest before the cruisewear show."

"*You* have forty minutes," Paisley said gaily. "*I* have the afternoon off—to spend with Gerard."

"You do?" Kelly's first reaction was jealousy. An afternoon off sounded like heaven. "If I had the afternoon off I could be with Chad. . . . Wait a minute. How did you get time off? No one asked me if I wanted a rest."

"You don't ask, you tell. I simply told someone to tell Loretta that I have terrible cramps and I'm going to have to stay in my room."

"You what? And she bought that?"

"No one told me no," Paisley said flippantly.

"Loretta couldn't care less about cramps, even if you did have them," Kelly exclaimed. "You know that—you're supposed to take aspirin and keep working. And what if Loretta calls the room to see how you're feeling? If you're not here she'll know you lied."

"Oh, who cares if she does? No one can work like this all day, every day. We deserve some time off."

"We did have the morning off."

"We did, but Gerard didn't, so it didn't help me any. I'm just changing my hours around a little bit. Don't worry so much."

"But I do worry!" Kelly exclaimed. "You're acting crazy, and if you keep it up, something drastic is going to happen. You'd better call Gerard and cancel your date."

"It's too late now," Paisley said cheerfully. "I'm meeting him downstairs in ten minutes."

"You can't," Kelly declared.

"I can and I am. They don't even need me for this cruisewear show. There are plenty of other girls." Paisley headed for the door, then stopped with her hand on the doorknob and gave Kelly a plaintive look. "You know how it is, Kelly," she said pleadingly. "You feel the same way about Chad. You'd be with him if you could—so don't be mad at me, okay? I'll see you later."

Kelly stared at the closed door, too astounded to know what to do. When the phone rang, she stared at that, too, then clenched her hands into fists and shook them, feeling as if she could scream.

"What is it," she growled into the receiver.

"Call for Miss Paisley Gregg," the operator answered.

"She's not here," Kelly snapped.

"She's not there, Mr. Renfrew," the operator repeated.

"Wait a minute," Kelly yelled, "did you say Mr. Renfrew? I'll take the call."

Chad's voice came over the line. "Sugar—is that you? Why did you say you weren't there?"

Silently, Kelly cursed herself for forgetting she was supposed to be Paisley Gregg! Things really *were* getting out of hand. "Uh, I—I didn't really hear her . . . these heavy accents . . ."

"Yeah, well, the reason I called is that I've just finished signing a contract for those feeders, so I thought I'd drop by for an hour or two later tonight, if you're not busy."

"I have a show from six to eight, but I could see you at nine. Is that all right?"

"These late hours are murder for a rancher," he said.

"Oh. I guess I understand." She felt a pang of keen disappointment.

"Hold on, I didn't say I wouldn't come, I just said it was tough. But you're worth it."

"Oh, Chad." Suddenly she didn't mind about Paisley so much. And maybe she'd tell Chad about her real name that night, when the time was right.

"That would be great," she said. "We could have dinner right here in the Galleria if you'd like, at one of the restaurants. Not in the hotel— I see Loretta and the models all day, it's nice to get away where no one recognizes me."

"Anything you want, Sugar. I'll call for you at nine. 'Bye."

"I should have told him to meet me at the restaurant," Kelly muttered as she hung up the phone.

Kelly waited expectantly near the front desk and anxiously scanned the lobby. She didn't want to meet anyone who knew her—except Chad. And there he was!

She smiled when she saw him. "Hi. You're right on time."

"You're worth hurrying for," he said.

"Well, um, let's get out of here," she said lightly, pulling him away from the desk.

They had a wonderful meal. She was becoming more comfortable with Chad's long silences. Besides, she had a lot to think about, waiting for the right moment to tell Chad her secret. But somehow the timing wasn't right. During dinner, Chad had told a long, funny story about his childhood. She didn't have the heart to spoil his good mood.

Then, over coffee, she decided to take the plunge. "Chad," she said hesitantly, "have you ever thought about people's names, how names influence the things they do?"

He smiled fondly at her. "You still thinking about those *C* names? Don't let that bother you, Sugar."

"Well, not really . . ."

Chad laughed. "You know, it *is* funny about names. I've just remembered—when I was really little, I had pet names for our horses. I forgot all about it till now. What were they . . ."

"Chad, I didn't mean horses' names," Kelly said impatiently. "I'm talking about people."

Chad waved his hand. "Hold on, don't talk now . . . I'm getting it. Something about hay, I think, or was it oats?"

"Chad . . ."

"Hush, Sugar; this is funny, if I can remember it." He bit his knuckle, concentrating. Idly, he glanced at his watch. "Yow, look at the time—I've got to be up at five A.M." He signaled the waitress for the check. "Don't worry, I know I'll remember those names, and I'll tell you next time. There will be a next time, won't there?"

Kelly sighed, giving up. Her secret would have to wait. "Well . . . of course."

He got up to go. "I'll walk you back to the hotel."

Obediently, she stood also. "You don't have to come in," she said as usual.

"I'd better. You get awfully nervous every time you have to go back there. I can understand it— you must be a little worried, being in a strange place by yourself at night. I'll make sure you get there safely."

She had to thank him for being so thoughtful.

I should have told him. But he didn't give me a chance. I'll have to tell him everything tomorrow.

Tuesday was another full day. Too full, Kelly told Paisley, catching her in the dressing room at their break. "I'm tired of lady shoppers, I'm tired of that endless runway, I'm tired of smiling and answering questions about clothes I know nothing about."

Paisley yawned and nodded. "Tell me about it."

"By the way, you look terrible," Kelly said. There was a thick layer of concealer under Paisley's eyes.

"Thanks," Paisley answered sarcastically. "I feel as good as I look."

"You were sick last night, weren't you? I wanted to ask you about it earlier, but you ran right into the bathroom this morning."

"I had a little beer last night and it didn't agree

with me. You know how Gerard is, he parties so hard and he loves me to keep up with him."

Kelly frowned. "Sure, because he thinks you're twenty-one. I don't suppose you told him your real name yet, did you?"

Paisley shrugged. "It never came up."

"We've got to do something," Kelly insisted. "At least we should talk about it, come up with an idea of what to do."

"Not now, please. I need a rest, okay? We'll talk later."

"Paisley . . ."

"Later." Paisley draped herself over a couch. She really did look sick.

Loretta hurried over to her. "There is a call for you, Paisley. It's Chad Renfrew. I knew his family. I didn't know you knew him."

Paisley's eyes drooped and she gave an impatient sigh. "He's very nice. But I'm too tired to talk—let Kelly take the call."

Loretta looked mystified. "Kelly? But he asked for you."

"That's okay, Loretta," Kelly said hastily, "we're all good friends. I'll take the call for Paisley—in my room, if that's okay."

Paisley's eyes were closed, so she missed the dirty look Kelly shot her as she hurried to their hotel room.

Chad sounded excited, as if he could hardly wait to talk to her. "How would you like to do something extra special tonight?" he asked.

"Sure—like what?"

"Like a sort of belated birthday party. You convinced me I ought to celebrate it after all."

She grinned; it was wonderful to hear him so happy. "Sounds great. When and what?"

"The usual time, I guess, nine o'clock. I've been away from the ranch all day, so I've got to get back and do a few things, but I've already called Skip and asked if he and Sunny would join us. Is that okay with you?"

"I'd rather be alone with you," she said wistfully.

"Oh." He sounded disappointed. "I just thought . . . a party, the more the merrier."

"Of course," she said quickly. "It's your birthday—a party is a wonderful idea."

"I thought we'd go to the country club up in River Oaks. It's pretty near you, so it won't be too late an evening. We're both so busy."

"Boy, you sure are thoughtful. Okay, I'll meet you outside, the usual place."

"I can come in and get you . . ."

"Not tonight, you have to park the car," she said vaguely. "I'll meet you outside at nine. See you then."

Thank goodness she'd brought her hot-pink outfit with her. She hadn't intended to take anything so fancy, but at the last minute a funny feeling had prompted her to pack it. A feeling about moonlight and strangers; Rochelle's prediction that she would meet a perfect stranger.

There was a knock on the door. When she answered it, a bellboy handed her a white florist's box with a card attached. Inside was a single white camellia. "A perfect flower for a perfect girl," the card said. It was signed, "Missing you already, Chad."

"Thank you," she cried, searching for her wallet. "Here!" She thrust three one-dollar bills into the boy's hand. "This is for you. Thanks so much!"

The flower had creamy white petals and a fragrance of romance. Dreamily, she held it up and peered in the mirror. It seemed to glow against her brown hair. Her eyes took on a soft and gentle look. She would wear the flower in her hair for their date tonight.

She stowed it carefully in the refrigerator to keep it fresh. Chad hadn't mentioned he ordered a flower when he spoke to her. He must have wanted to surprise her. He really was incredibly thoughtful. If anyone was perfect, it was Chad!

An image of Eric's deep blue eyes, his special smile, came to her suddenly. But she shook her head indignantly.

He has a nerve; Chad missed me after one afternoon apart. Eric hasn't missed me in four days. He could have called if he was sorry.

But Eric can be sweet, too, she thought wistfully, remembering the time they'd cooked dinner together at his house. He had toasted her with soda as if it were wine, and they'd kissed. . . .

But what about him choosing a hockey game over my skating party? He isn't thoughtful, he's just completely, absolutely selfish! Chad would never do a thing like that to me!

There was no comparison. She couldn't imagine Eric dealing with agents and ranchhands and staff—impossible! Eric was a child. Chad was grown-up, an adult. He made her feel grown-up herself.

Of course, Chad never kids around like Eric does. But that's dumb. You can't enjoy being childish and grown-up at the same time!

Annoyed at herself, she stood up and hurried out of the room. There was no good reason to think about Eric, not as long as someone like Chad wanted her.

Ten

At dinner, Chad turned to Kelly and remarked, "You never told me why you didn't get an afternoon off, like Sunny had."

"She didn't really have it off," Kelly admitted. "She took it off, for . . . illness." She avoided Paisley's eyes. Paisley seemed to have perked up since the afternoon, and she was sure to be angry at being caught in a lie. *But I can't have Chad thinking I had the chance to see him and chose not to!* she thought.

Gerard dropped his fork onto the creamy linen tablecloth, looking alarmed. "Were you sick?"

Paisley gazed at the group of people at the next table. "Hush, Gerard, I wasn't really sick." She glared at Kelly. "I just wanted to be with you so, actually, I kind of faked it."

Gerard frowned in disapproval. "I want to be with you too, Sunshine, but it's always best to be honest."

Paisley smirked. "Come on, Gerard, you had a great time yesterday. What difference does it make what I had to tell Loretta?"

"I just don't cotton to lyin'. It goes against my code of honor. My family never lies."

Chad put his hand over Kelly's. "Speaking of families, you haven't told me much about your family, Sugar. What are they like? What do you all do together?"

"Oh, nothing special," Kelly said evasively, feeling sneaky. *It's Paisley's fault I have to lie to Chad. Darn Paisley, anyway!*

"Let's drink to family honor," Gerard cried heartily. He lifted his champagne glass.

"Are you sure you should do that?" Kelly said sharply as Paisley took a mouthful, swallowed, and giggled.

"It's a birthday party," Gerard boomed. "Time to make merry. And you, little lady," he said to Kelly as he refilled his glass, "are the only one underage."

Except for Paisley, who lied to you, she said to herself.

Paisley giggled and lifted Gerard's hand, holding his champagne glass to her mouth. She drank the champagne as if it were water.

"You ought to watch that," Kelly said.

"What's the big deal?"

"Word could get back to the Noireau people. You shouldn't risk *your* good name."

Gerard looked at Kelly quizzically. "If Sunny

isn't worried, why should you be? What Sunny does doesn't affect you."

Kelly pursed her mouth and wadded her napkin into a ball. "Let's go to the ladies' room, Sunny. Now." She pushed back her chair, and Paisley reluctantly followed to the restroom.

"What's got into you, Blake? I thought we were all having a good time."

"Look, Paisley, how about cooling it? Loretta would be furious if she heard you were drinking—illegally."

"How would Loretta know what I did tonight? Unless you tell her, but even you aren't that stupid."

"Use your brains—half the women here tonight are regulars at the Galleria events. They could say something to Loretta."

Paisley dismissed her. "They're not going to tell, because they couldn't care less. Why are you picking on me?"

Kelly closed her eyes, feeling drained by it all. "Maybe I am picking on you, but it's only because this whole thing is making me crazy! Paisley, let's just tell the boys our real names. It's stupid not to. The only one who cares is Meg Dorian."

Paisley grabbed her arms. "No, you don't understand. If you tell now it will completely ruin things for me."

"But I can't stand it anymore," Kelly exploded. "I have to watch everything I say." She rubbed her temples. "It's giving me a headache."

"You can't tell them yet," Paisley begged.

Kelly's voice was a tense shriek. "Gerard probably won't even care. Blame the whole thing on Meg Dorian. Say she doesn't like you to be a live wire, he'll understand."

Paisley fidgeted. "You heard Gerard about his code of honor. I don't know what he'll do if he finds out I lied to him all along."

"Then you've got to tell him, the sooner the better," Kelly urged. "Putting it off will only make it worse. I can't take it. I'm terrified I'll call you Paisley instead of Sunny."

Paisley groaned. "I just can't confess. Maybe you could—that's the kind of thing you can do, but I just can't. I wouldn't even know how to begin."

"Then let me tell them both. At least let me try—I'll shut up if it looks like the wrong thing to do."

"No, are you crazy? You can't start a scene here!"

"One of us has to," Kelly said firmly.

"No!" Paisley grabbed at her to hold her back, but Kelly wrestled away.

Gerard watched suspiciously as they approached the table, Kelly standing grim and determined, Paisley wringing her hands anxiously.

"Something strange is going on, I've got this funny feeling," he said.

Paisley looked sick as she sank onto her chair. Kelly sat resolutely, taking a deep breath for courage.

"Nothing's wrong," she said bravely. "In fact, we were just discussing your code of honor, Gerard. I—I really admire that. I didn't know you cared about things like that."

Chad smiled at her indulgently. "Well, you haven't spent as much time with Skip as you have with me, Sugar."

"Let me talk," she snapped, afraid she would lose her nerve. "I was thinking, it just shows how you can know a person but yet not really know them . . ."

Chad laughed and laid his hand over Kelly's. "What dark secret are you hiding from me, Sugar?"

Kelly squirmed. Paisley gave her a pleading glance.

Abruptly, Kelly stood up. "Let's dance."

Chad hurried after her onto the dance floor. "You're awfully edgy tonight. I've never seen you this way before."

"You've never seen me any way," she snapped in frustration. "We hardly even talk to each other, except for your giving me compliments all the time."

Chad pulled back in surprise. "Something is wrong with you." He looked hurt. "Did I do something wrong, offend you somehow . . ."

"You didn't do anything. Can't I be . . . not perfect sometimes? I'm not always smiling and perky every minute. I'm not perfect, you know."

Chad whistled softly. "You're really in a stew about something, Sugar. Maybe it's that contest tomorrow."

"I'm not in a stew," she said sharply. "I'm not . . . Oh, forget it. Let's sit down."

Chad shrugged and followed her to the table.

"Back so soon?" Gerard looked at them in surprise.

Kelly frowned. "I didn't recognize that music they're playing. Maybe it's because there are no young people here but us."

Chad and Gerard exchanged a look. "There are more young people on weekends," Chad said. "Don't worry. That's the time we'd mostly be here ourselves. Ranchwomen save up their partying for the end of the week, and this is about the best place to come. My folks came here every weekend."

Kelly looked around at the groups of people greeting each other, exchanging little kisses on the cheek, very proper and reserved.

"That sounds a little—limited," she said. "Coming here every weekend to see the same people, over and over."

"This is Houston," Gerard boomed, "just a big small town. Everyone knows everyone else. At least, all the right people know all the other right people."

Kelly gave him a withering look. "I thought you liked lively places," she said sarcastically.

Gerard scratched his head. "Sure I do, but this is where the money goes. Chad and I have to keep up contacts, too, otherwise society forgets you."

"Society?"

Chad leaned closer to Kelly. "That stuff isn't important to everyone, I know, but it's important to me. I like fitting in. But don't worry, Sugar, you'd fit right in too; you'd be as charming as my mother was. She always gathered a good crowd at our table on weekends."

Suddenly Kelly felt as though she couldn't

breathe. She picked up her napkin and began fanning herself. "It's awfully stuffy in here. It's much too hot."

"Sit quietly and try to breathe slowly." Chad hovered over her, concerned. "You've been working too hard. You ought to take it easy."

Kelly leaned away from him, feeling like a complaining child but unable to stop herself. "It's not from working, for crying out loud; I'm not an old lady. I like being active. I used to run track and cross-country, did you know that? If anything, I'm not getting enough exercise."

Paisley cut in quickly. "You'd get plenty of exercise on a ranch, wouldn't she, Chad?"

Kelly relented a little. "It would be nice to ride anytime I wanted to, with all that wide-open space around."

"Sure it would," Chad said soothingly, "but mostly you'd be inside, supervising the household. My mother mostly stayed inside."

Kelly clenched her hands into fists. "I am not your mother," she shouted. There was a tense silence.

"How about this Noireau contest," Paisley said brightly. "I bet our Sugar has it in the bag. I'm almost positive."

Gerard patted her hand. "Now, Sunny, don't be so modest yourself. I'm not tryin' to start a fight between you gals, but you have as good a chance of winnin' as Sugar here."

"I'd like to win," Paisley said wistfully. "It would certainly help my modeling career, but even more important, after I was Miss Noireau I could really get backing for my fashion designs.

That's my true ambition, after all. Someday, my design firm will be as famous as the House of Noireau."

"You really have spunk, don't you, Sunny?" Gerard was impressed.

"Yes, but that won't help me win this contest," Paisley said sadly. "If it was anyone else but Sugar who won, I'd be jealous. All that exposure and publicity, and money of course, and the traveling—you get to go everywhere."

Chad looked at Kelly. "Is that true? You'd do a lot of traveling?"

"That's the best part," Paisley told him. "The winner gets to go to Paris three times a year for the new collections."

Chad folded his arms across his chest. "Are you sure that's what you want? It sounds awfully tiring to me. Seems a woman should spend her time at home, where she belongs."

Kelly threw down her napkin and took a deep breath. Sensing disaster, Paisley sprang to her feet. "Chad, let's dance," she cried hastily. "This is my favorite song. Come on."

She tried to drag Chad onto the dance floor, but Chad held back, fussing over Kelly. "I shouldn't leave her," he protested. "She's upset about something."

Kelly put her hands to her temples. "Please stop fighting over me! I—I have a terrible headache. I think we'd better go back to the hotel, Chad. I'm sorry."

Chad went to her immediately, his face somber with concern. "I knew you weren't yourself. Of course I'll take you back. But . . . before we go, while we're all together . . ."

"Well, what is it?"

"I wanted to ask you to go to the Miss Noireau ball with me. Skip already asked Sunny, and, well, I wanted us all to go together."

"Sure, we can all go together," she said, without much enthusiasm.

Chad looked so sweet, so worried. Suddenly she felt awful about the way she was acting. "Chad, I wouldn't go with anyone else but you."

Chad breathed a sigh of relief.

"I'm glad that's settled," she said. She turned to Paisley. "Now are you ready to go?"

"Me—go?" Paisley looked startled. "I don't have a headache. I'm going to stay here with Gerard."

"I thought we'd all go," Kelly said. "I thought you'd want to get in on time tonight."

"We won't stay too late," Paisley insisted. "Go ahead, you go on—I'll be there soon."

Kelly gave up.

In the car, Chad played the radio softly. "I'm sorry we had to leave early," he said after a few miles, "but I'm glad to be alone with you."

Kelly agreed. Now that they'd left the country club she felt more like herself again. Chad grasped her hand. His eyes were dark and soft, and the passing highway lights threw deep shadows on his face. He looked very handsome.

She smiled gently. "I'm sorry if I spoiled the party. I got . . . upset, about a lot of things."

Chad looked at her, then pulled the car into a

rest area at the side of the road and turned off the engine. "I'm sorry, too," he said earnestly. "I didn't mean to compare you to my mother. I—I can't help it, somehow. I know you can't expect people to be anything but what they already are; I know you have to take them for themselves. But that's why it's so . . . unbelievable that you're the way you are. You're wonderful. I know you're not perfect—no one's perfect. I just meant you're perfect for me."

He leaned over, searching her eyes intently. "I'm in love with you," he said. "I—I think I really love you."

A shiver ran through Kelly's body. "Oh, Chad, I . . ."

But before she could finish her thought, Chad bent his head close to hers. "Hush," he said gently, "hush—don't say a word." His eyes closed and Kelly closed her eyes, too. She felt his lips brush against hers in a soft, gentle kiss.

Kelly forgot the reason for her bad mood; her headache vanished. Chad pulled away, a wondering look on his face. "I never thought I'd find a girl like you. I—I only hoped I would." He kissed her again, even more softly. He took her hand in his.

"I've been so lonely sometimes." He pulled her close. "I need you, Sugar." He folded his arms around her tightly and rocked her gently. "Let's just sit here a while. We'll go home in a minute, I promise."

He held her so quietly. It was almost as if she could feel his loneliness, and her heart ached for him.

"Do you think you could . . . love me, too?"

"Oh, Chad, I . . ." Her heart melted at the look in his eyes. "Yes—yes, I could. If I had more time . . ."

He kissed her again and she felt like laughing and crying at the same time. She pulled away, breathless. "I never felt this way about anyone," she said. "Oh, Chad, I'm so sorry I acted so bratty before. It's just that . . ."

"Hush—you don't need to explain to me." He kissed her again until her heart was pounding. Then he pulled away.

"Whoa—hold on, now. If we don't stop now, we never will," he joked softly. "And then you'll miss your curfew."

"I don't care about curfew," she declared. "I'd rather be with you." She tried to kiss him, but he held her off. She felt a pang of annoyance; hadn't he just said he loved her? Who cared about curfews at a time like this?

"No, Sugar, this contest means a lot to you, and I'm not going to do anything to ruin your chances to win. If I did, you'd only resent me."

"Well, that makes sense, I guess." Reluctantly, she brushed back her hair and snapped her seat belt back on. Then, impulsively, she bent over and hugged him.

"Hey, what's that for?" He looked really pleased.

"I guess you deserve it," Kelly said. "I mean, it's really sweet of you to worry about me winning the contest. I know you don't approve of it."

"It's because I care for you." He kissed her

forehead, then her eyelids. "Don't think it isn't hard for me to leave you now," he said. "But we have to do the responsible thing, don't we?"

"Sure, of course we do."

Chad started the car. "I can't wait to see you tomorrow night. You're not tired of seeing me every night, are you?"

Feeling wise and womanly Kelly placed a finger over his lips. "Of course not."

"I want to know everything about you, Sugar. The way you think and feel about everything . . ."

"You will," Kelly said uneasily. "Don't worry, you will."

Paisley leaned into the bathroom mirror, applying layers of concealer to the circles under her eyes. She groaned. "I feel horrible. How could champagne taste so good when it makes you feel like this the day after?" Shakily, she put on more concealer.

"Paisley, that looks terrible. Rolf will only have to remove it to do your makeup today."

Paisley sighed in despair. "Your makeup artist knows everything, doesn't he?" She threw down the concealer stick in disgust. "Listen, Kelly, thanks for not saying I told you so."

"I guess you've been punished enough." Kelly yawned, pulling on her jeans. "And I'm glad we could sleep late this morning."

"I'm just glad this job is almost over. Just think, Kelly, tonight you'll win the contest, and then everything will be easy again."

Kelly suddenly sat straight up. "The contest," she gasped. "They'll announce the winner at the Miss Noireau Ball."

"So?"

"So Chad and Gerard will be at the ball."

"I know that." Paisley stared at her as if she were crazy.

"So think about it—suppose I do win? They'll announce my name, Kelly Blake, and I'll have to go get the award. As me, as Kelly Blake. Chad and Gerard will know then, won't they?"

Paisley's mouth dropped open in horror. "Oh, my gosh, you're right. How could I be so stupid, not to have thought of that." She pulled her short hair in despair.

"It'll be awful," Kelly groaned. "We can't go through with it. We'll have to cancel our dates."

"We can't. They'd come anyway. Besides, I think Gerard is planning something really special. There must be some other way. There must be something we can do."

Kelly closed her eyes and swallowed hard. "We have to tell them the truth before the contest, then. There's no other way."

Paisley wailed, "Gerard will be furious, and then he'll never ask me."

"Ask you what?" Kelly eyed Paisley suspiciously. "What's he going to ask you?"

"Nothing." Paisley was suddenly evasive.

"Paisley, you don't think he'd going to ask you to—to marry him, or something like that?" She stared at her, incredulous.

Paisley became defensive. "Why not? Chad has hinted as much to you."

"That's crazy. I mean, Chad has a reason to want someone, he's all alone on that ranch. But Gerard is still in college, he wouldn't want to settle down."

"I didn't say we'd settle down right away," Paisley protested. "But we could get engaged. Besides, people marry young in Texas."

"But you have plans; you have a career."

"I won't have much of a career without any money to finance it," Paisley grumbled.

Kelly's eyes narrowed. "You wouldn't really marry Gerard just for his money. Even you couldn't do that."

"It's not just that," Paisley protested. "I really like Gerard. I think—I think I'm in love with him. He's so different from any boy I've ever dated."

"He's not so different that he wants to get married or engaged. I can tell."

"You don't know that for sure. He's crazy about me, and I like him, too. I wouldn't spend all my time with him if I didn't. He's—he's tons of fun." Paisley began to pace restlessly. "This is awful. If Gerard finds out I lied, he'll never want to see me again. I know it. It'll ruin everything."

"Come on, Paisley, you knew something like this would happen. It was inevitable. Let's tell them the truth."

"But I thought I'd fix things somehow. I still can; I'll think of something, I swear it."

Kelly watched her closely. "Do you care for Gerard at all?"

Paisley became very still. "Of course I do," she

said solemnly. "I really do. You have to believe me."

Why do I always give in? Kelly sighed. "All right, Paisley, but you'd better come up with an idea soon. I can't take much more of this!"

"I will," Paisley cried gratefully. "Thank you, you're the most wonderful friend I ever had. You're the *only* friend I ever had." Paisley grabbed Kelly and hugged her. Then she stood back, embarrassed.

"I know I'm not the easiest person to get along with," she said haltingly. "But I just want you to know how much I appreciate what you're doing for me. You're the first girlfriend I've ever trusted like this."

She was obviously sincere, and Kelly was moved. *But now I absolutely can't tell Chad the truth. Why is everything so complicated?*

Eleven

Only one modeling event was scheduled for that day—informal modeling of loungewear—before the contest. When Kelly and Paisley arrived downstairs, the other models were already backstage getting dressed.

"Hurry up, girls," Loretta urged them. "Kelly—may I have a word with you?"

"With me?"

Loretta drew her aside and looked at her sternly. "I have been going over the sign-in sheets. The desk clerk verifies the time you girls sign in, and Kelly Blake has signed in late every night this week. Not just a few minutes, either, but significantly late. You are not bound by contract to be in by curfew, but it *is* part of your responsibility to your job."

Kelly fidgeted uncomfortably. She hadn't been getting in late; it was Paisley, signing her name. But she couldn't tell Loretta that. "Believe me, Loretta, I had good reason to be late."

Loretta frowned. "You are a fine model, but word gets around in this business. You have always had a good reputation before, as a cooperative and responsible model, and I would hate to see that change. I assume you have met someone."

"Yes," Kelly admitted. *At least that part was true.* "Someone wonderful."

"He had better be wonderful. He could cost you a lot."

As Loretta turned away, Michelle passed by, gloating. "I had such a lovely dinner with Miss DeFarge last night. I could tell she really liked me."

"With DeFarge? How?" Kelly demanded.

"Did you not know? There was a notice about it at the desk. All the models were invited. Too bad you missed it. It gave me a chance to really impress her with my poise. Poise is crucial for Miss Noireau, you know. After all, she is more than just a model, she is an ambassador."

Kelly hadn't seen the note, but then she hadn't stopped at the desk, she was in such a hurry to meet Chad.

"Do not take it too hard," Michelle said, "it could not have been *that* important to DeFarge's final decision."

Darn, Kelly thought, *and darn Michelle for rubbing it in.* Quickly, she pulled on the roomy lounging pajamas she was assigned to wear.

Paisley was already busy admiring her Noireau sunsuit in the dressing room mirror.

"Not bad," she said, adjusting the low-cut top. "I'd like one of these myself, wouldn't you, Kelly? It gives me that European air."

"I wouldn't worry about that if I were you," Kelly said sourly. "The Miss Noireau Ball is only a few hours away, and you haven't come up with any plan yet."

"I will, I will. Plenty of time left."

Loretta cleared her throat. "Attention, girls. Let me repeat your instructions. When you hear your name, you are to walk down the runway, turn twice, then descend the steps into the audience and circulate through the crowd. I want you close enough for those ladies to reach out and feel the fabric."

"And see the circles under my eyes," Paisley muttered.

"Remember, listen to the commentator for your cue, girls. Have a good show, and smile, smile, smile!"

Kelly took a deep breath. "Why am I always so nervous?"

"Don't worry, this is a piece of cake." Paisley fussed with her hair. "How do I look?"

"Great, and there's your cue, Paisley! Good luck!"

Kelly gave Paisley a little shove toward the curtains. They could hear the commentator announce: "And here's Paisley, ready for a day by the pool in her favorite sunsuit."

Flashing Kelly a bright smile, Paisley pulled back the curtains, took one step, then gasped.

"Oh, no!" Her face went white under her makeup. She whipped the curtains closed.

Kelly stared at her in amazement. "What are you doing? Get out there!"

Paisley gulped. "I can't. Gerard is out there. And Chad is with him."

"You're crazy, that's impossible." Kelly pushed the curtains aside an inch. "Chad had work to do today, he couldn't be here . . ." She poked her head through the opening and gasped herself. Her eyes widened in alarm. "You're not crazy. It's them. What are they doing here? What are we going to do?" She reached down and ripped a tag off her shirt. It said "Kelly Blake—Noireau #271, lounging pajamas."

Paisley ripped off her own tag. Outside, there was a rustling sound as the audience stirred. The commentator cleared her throat, improvising. "Paisley is making sure that sunsuit is perfect before she appears in public—just like you and me, ladies." The audience laughed.

Paisley was in a complete panic. "I can't go out there. I'm going to be sick again."

"Don't just stand there," Kelly cried. "Do something!"

"You've got to go before me!" Paisley shoved Kelly through the curtains.

As the commentator looked up in startled confusion, Kelly stumbled onto the stage, catching herself and flashing an unsteady smile.

"Uh, Paisley seems to have changed outfits," the woman stuttered.

Composing herself, Kelly spun and began her walk down the runway. From the corner of her eye, she spotted Chad and Gerard in the crowd. Pretending to be pleasantly surprised, she nodded their way, then resumed her walk toward the audience.

The runway felt about five miles long. Her heart was pounding. She could see Elise De-Farge in the audience, frowning in disapproval. Kelly's heart sank. There was no way she could explain this. She could kick herself. Meanwhile, Chad was trying to catch her eye. Deliberately, she turned away from him as she descended the steps, and walked through the audience on the other side of the room.

There was a low murmur from the audience. The commentator stammered a feeble explanation. "Well, Paisley forgot her sunsuit, but doesn't she look nice in her lounging pajamas, anyway?" While the audience tolerantly applauded, the woman hurriedly looked through her notes.

The commentator collected herself and began reading the next introduction: "And here's Kelly, looking carefree and casual in her stunning day pajamas . . ." Paisley dove through the curtains in her sunsuit.

The audience tittered. "Well," the commentator stumbled, "uh, here's Kelly after all—or is it Paisley—in that sunsuit I told you about."

There were snickers of laughter, but Paisley smiled grandly, bluffing her way through the ordeal. At the foot of the stairs she took an abrupt left turn, and followed Kelly down the other side of the plaza, away from the boys.

Behind her, the commentator had recovered

her composure, and the other girls were parading out on cue. There were no more snags as the models circulated through the crowd.

"All we have to do now is keep away from Loretta, Chad, and Gerard," Paisley muttered at Kelly through clenched teeth.

A woman reached up, trying to touch Kelly's billowy sleeves, and Kelly leaned over so the woman could feel the fabric. "I thought you were going to take care of this mess," she hissed over her shoulder.

"I haven't thought of the right plan yet," Paisley defended herself.

"DeFarge saw the whole thing, you know," Kelly said, moving on through the crowd. "She'll think I'm a complete idiot now, on top of missing her dinner last night, and being bawled out by Loretta. It's a complete disaster. I'll never be Miss Noireau now!"

Paisley grabbed her shoulder. "Watch out," she hissed, "Gerard and Chad are headed our way."

"Move—run," Kelly blurted. She and Paisley hurried through the crowd. Kelly bent over a man and woman at the nearest table. "Have you ever seen such stunning lounging pajamas? Just feel that fabric."

Then she whipped over to the next table. "You appreciate fine workmanship, don't you, Ma'am?"

Paisley gulped. "Loretta is heading this way," she cried faintly.

"Do something," Kelly spat out desperately.

Paisley looked from Loretta to Chad and Gerard. "Oh . . . I feel faint!" With a dramatic moan, Paisley swooned, dropping backward onto the small table. The woman seated there jumped back, shrieking.

Grabbing a napkin, Kelly leaned over Paisley, fanning her face. "Now what?"

"Let's get out of here," Paisley whispered.

"Uh, don't talk now, uh—save your strength." Kelly pulled the limp Paisley to a sitting position on the table.

Loretta hurried toward them. "Look, if she's ill . . ."

"I'll handle it, Loretta," Kelly said. "Excuse me." Propping Paisley against her, Kelly pushed through the crowd around the table, and she and Paisley scurried away from the plaza.

"I can't believe this," Paisley sputtered. "I can't believe I did that!" Wild giggles erupted from her mouth. Kelly tried to hold back her own laughter, but it bubbled up. She exploded, laughing until her side hurt.

"Get that elevator," Paisley shrieked, doubling over in a giggling fit. The elevator doors slid shut—they were safe!

"Ow, it hurts," Kelly moaned, clutching her side. "Stop laughing!"

"I can't stop—until you stop," Paisley choked.

Gasping for breath, Kelly pulled Paisley off at their floor, running for the safety of their room. She slammed the door behind them.

"We made it; we're safe," Paisley yelled, collapsing onto her bed.

Kelly wiped tears from her eyes, sobering up. "Safe, except I just blew all my chances with Elise DeFarge. I saw her looking at us as if we were lunatics." She sighed, feeling hollow inside.

Her laughter was all gone. "It would be funny if it weren't so tragic." She threw herself on the bed next to Paisley.

"I thought Loretta would strangle me," Paisley confessed. "She knew I was faking."

"Where did you get that fainting act from, anyway?"

"Southern belles always used to faint."

"Yeah, but this isn't the Old South. You were ridiculous!"

"I didn't see you coming up with any better ideas. At least we got away."

Kelly looked down at her outfit. "Sure, we escaped in our Noireau loungewear. One of us has to take these clothes downstairs to the dressing room, and it's not going to be me."

Paisley moaned. "We can send a bellboy. I'm not showing my face around here until the ball."

"That's a great idea. I'll call the front desk." Kelly spoke briefly into the phone. "They're sending one right now. Come on, let's get these clothes off before we're accused of robbery on top of everything else."

Kelly dropped her pajama bottoms on the floor. The phone rang. "What now?" She grabbed the phone, thinking it was about the bellboy. Her eyes widened in alarm. "It's Chad," she whispered to Paisley. "Hi, Chad . . . She's much better. No, she didn't really faint, ha, ha." She gave Paisley a sickly look. ". . . but she was feeling sick all morning. It happens to models all the time—anxiety attacks, you know."

Paisley put her hand over the receiver. "Tell him to tell Gerard I'm feeling much better now."

Kelly shrugged her away. "Yes, she's better now, thanks. Sure, our date for the ball is still on. Right, Paisley and Gerard's, too. We'll see you later, Chad."

As soon as Kelly hung up, a knock came at the door. "Oh, there's the bellboy," she announced, removing her pajama jacket and pulling on a robe. "Give me your sunsuit." Paisley threw it at her. Ignoring her, Kelly opened the door. "Loretta!"

"It's showdown time, girls," Loretta announced grimly, closing the door behind her. "Suppose you tell me what is going on."

Paisley licked her lips nervously, sitting up. "Well, I, uh . . ."

"It was an honest mistake," Kelly blurted. "A—a mix-up. You see, Paisley mislaid one of her shoes, and I had to change places with her on the runway. I had to—she couldn't go out with one shoe on."

"You should have told an assistant or myself," Loretta said angrily.

"There wasn't time," Kelly pleaded. "Honestly, the shoe, uh, fell off at the last minute and we couldn't find it anywhere, so I had to go first. It was the lesser of two evils. Either me in the wrong place, or Paisley hobbling on one shoe . . ."

Loretta made a disgusted sound. "I do not understand. I had such good reports on you from Meg Dorian. But you two have given me more trouble than all the other girls combined."

Kelly swallowed deeply. "Loretta, will this

hurt me with Miss DeFarge—I mean, if she was considering me for Miss Noireau?"

"I don't know," Loretta said sharply. "If it were me, it would." She fixed Paisley with a poisonous glare. "And how about you. Were your shoes so tight they made you faint? What was that ridiculous act all about?"

Paisley looked pained. "Well, I, uh . . ."

"It really wasn't her fault, Loretta," Kelly pleaded. "She panicked with the shoe business and she just . . . fainted."

"There is a right way and wrong way to handle things." Loretta went to the door. "This promotion has nearly ended. I hope you will fulfill your remaining duties without any more 'mix-ups'. Miss DeFarge's interest may . . ." She stopped suddenly.

"I knew it," Paisley whooped. "I knew it— DeFarge is interested in you, Kelly. What did she say, Loretta?"

Loretta frowned. "I've said too much already. But a word to the wise, girls. I did have to report your behavior to Meg Dorian."

"You didn't!" Paisley, on the bed, collapsed again, but this time for real.

"Oh, yes," Loretta said calmly. "You and Kelly are the youngest models here. You have been given adult privileges, but you have not lived up to the responsibility. That will not do—not for this assignment, not for any assignment."

"I understand," Kelly said meekly.

"Good. Because I have enough to do without being a baby-sitter."

"Yes, Loretta."

Loretta closed the door firmly behind her. Paisley scrunched her pillow into a ball and punched it viciously. "She called Meg! All that sneaking around, pretending to be you, for nothing. I'm ruined!"

Twelve

"*You* are ruined?" Kelly stared at Paisley. "*You're* not ruined, *I* am! According to the sign-in sheets, Kelly Blake is the one who signed in late every night. Loretta told Meg about *me*, not you!"

Paisley slowly smiled. "You're right! Oh, Kelly, honey, I'm sorry. But let's face it—Meg will forgive you."

"What? You think Loretta didn't tell Meg how you've insulted her all week, and how you missed one fashion show? We've both got some explaining to do."

Paisley's face fell. "Oh. Well, at least she'll be mad at both of us. Boy, if Meg thinks you're bad, too, she won't take it out so much on me. You're never bad."

"Can't you take the blame yourself for once?"

"But every time something happens here you blame it on me," Paisley complained.

"Who else should I blame it on?" Kelly screeched. "Meg thinks I've been running wild, and I haven't even *done* anything! All because of you, Miss Sunny. And I'm so sick of that phony name, if I hear it one more time I'm going to scream!"

"Oh, and I'm supposed to love little saccharine-sweet Sugar, the world's biggest hypocrite?"

"What hypocrite? I haven't done anything hypocritical."

Paisley threw her head back and laughed. "Oh, no? What do you call letting Chad believe you're the sweetest little homemaker this side of the Rockies?"

"I've never been dishonest with Chad. I never said one thing I didn't believe. I love his ranch, anybody would love it."

"Oh, right—who do you think you're kidding? You're just as ambitious as I am. The only one who doesn't know that is Chad. He wouldn't want the *real* you, and the *real* Kelly Blake would hate being stuck on some dull ranch."

"I *am* the real Kelly Blake, and I know what I want!"

"Well, you'd better tell Chad what that is. His mother married young—and he wants you to be exactly like her."

"That's ridiculous." Kelly laughed nervously. "Come on, he knows I wouldn't consider that, not yet, anyway."

"You're leading him on; you're being a hypocrite."

For a second, Kelly felt horribly uneasy. Then she felt a helpless fury. "I know one thing," she spat at Paisley. "I'll never do a so-called friend a favor like this again—never in my entire life!"

She slammed into the bathroom and started water running noisily in the tub. She was furious with Paisley. Unbelievably furious! There wasn't a grain of truth in what she'd said.

Paisley pounded on the closed door. "It's true," she yelled. "Do you hear me? You're just as much a phony as I am!"

Kelly didn't answer. A minute later she heard the door to the room slam. Peeking out of the bathroom, she saw that Paisley had gone. Probably chasing after Gerard—and she probably wouldn't find him.

She's wrong. It's not true.

Turning off the water in the tub, she picked up the telephone. Slowly, she dialed a number.

The phone was picked up on the second ring. Kelly took a deep breath and swallowed. "Jennifer? Hi, it's me."

"Kelly! How are you," Jennifer cried, as if nothing was wrong.

For a second, Kelly was speechless. "I'm fine, thanks . . . but, I thought we were mad at each other."

"Why?" Jennifer laughed in her usual straightforward way. "What would I be mad at you about?"

"Campy's," Kelly said. "I yelled at you, don't you remember? I've been thinking about it all week. I got mad when you didn't take my side of the argument."

"Oh, that." Jennifer sounded apologetic. "You know I'm like that. I always see an argument from both sides. I didn't think you'd be mad at me about it."

"But I thought you were mad at *me*. You wouldn't answer your phone when I called you later."

"My family left to visit my cousins that night. You know how my father prefers to drive when the roads are empty. I told you we were going. We didn't get back until late Sunday."

Kelly smacked a hand against her forehead. "You did tell me. I completely forgot. And all this time I thought you were angry."

"Why would I be?" Jennifer spoke briskly. "So how's it going; how's the big-time competition? It must be really exciting."

"Well, yeah . . . Oh, Jen, I miss all you guys."

"We miss you, too! Listen, I really hate to do this to you, but I have to run. Some kids from computer science class are getting together to work on this *awful* assignment and Jamie Flaherty is outside now, honking away. I can't wait for you to get home! Call me if you win that contest, okay? Promise."

"I promise."

"Great. I know you'll win. 'Bye."

Kelly stared at the phone. She hadn't told Jennifer about Chad—or asked about Eric! Eric—she'd promised herself not to think about him. It was too confusing. *I'm just going to concentrate on winning the contest,* she decided. *I won't think about Chad till I see him again tonight.* But it didn't work. Every time she pushed her thoughts of Chad away, an image of Eric appeared.

Chad twirled Kelly expertly. Her emerald-green taffeta crinkled and swished around her, but her smile remained tight and stiff.

Chad held her away from him, frowning. "What's wrong with you tonight, Sugar? You won't talk to me, you won't look at me . . . and you look so beautiful in that dress."

Kelly couldn't speak. The lump in her throat felt as if it were the size of an orange. She must have been crazy to let things go this far without telling Chad the truth. Here they were, at the Miss Noireau Ball, with disaster minutes away, but still she couldn't tell him. How could she, with him mooning over her, telling her how beautiful and how perfect she was, telling her that he loved her.

She shook her head helplessly, tears welling in her eyes. "I can't," she choked.

"Sugar, please. Tell me what's wrong. If you're worried about the contest, I'm telling you you're the prettiest girl here."

Paisley was at the table with Gerard, looking as ill at ease as Kelly. The Galleria had been transformed into a magic ballroom, with fountains spurting, flowers everywhere, and violins playing—but neither Kelly nor Paisley could enjoy it at all.

"This is some night," Gerard said, as Kelly and Chad sat down. "All the beautiful people. Everyone who's anyone, society and fashion folks. Quite a night."

Paisley nodded mutely.

Chad turned and called hello to someone he knew. "There are the Schnabels; come on, Sugar, I'll introduce you."

"No, no, not right now," she protested. "I just don't want to meet any of your friends."

Chad and Gerard exchanged baffled looks and impatient glances. Kelly looked at Paisley, hoping she could help, but Paisley looked positively ill, as tongue-tied and miserable as Kelly. Gerard seemed fed up and angry.

"I don't get it," he fumed. "First you stalled gettin' down here, now you won't talk—what's the matter with the two of you?"

"I . . . we . . . you—" Paisley stuttered. She was interrupted by a drumroll. The house lights dimmed, and Loretta appeared on the stage, microphone in hand.

"I hate to interrupt," Loretta announced, "but there is a reason we are all here, and it's time to get to it." She took a breath, and the room hushed expectantly. "Ladies and gentlemen, Miss Elise DeFarge from Paris, France, representing the House of Noireau."

There was loud applause, and Elise, stunning in deep blue velvet, took the·microphone. *"Merci beaucoup*, thank you," she said graciously, her accent lilting over the words. She began to explain the Noireau philosophy of beauty. Kelly, wringing her napkin between her hands, heard as though through a fog.

". . . independent . . . feminine yet strong . . . bold yet refined . . ."

That's me, I know it, Kelly thought. Someone tapped her shoulder, and she looked up into Michelle Chalfonte's blue eyes. "Not now, Michelle," she groaned.

"I thought I would sit at the winner's table," Michelle gushed, eyeing Chad openly. "It is you or me," she told Kelly. "And I just hope it is me."

Chad clapped his hand over Kelly's. "Don't worry," he said gently. "Michelle doesn't stand a chance next to you."

Kelly nodded, feeling sick—from nerves over the contest, and from anxiety. What would Chad do when he heard her real name announced?

". . . thanks also to the heads of some of the world's leading modeling agencies."

Several people stood in the audience, among them a tall, no-nonsense-looking woman with striking features and short-cropped, salt-and-pepper hair.

"Meg!" Paisley gasped. Kelly grabbed her water glass, gulping mouthfuls. "What's she doing here?"

"She didn't say she was coming," Kelly said weakly. Her hands began to sweat and the blood rushed to her head. Chad looked at her queerly, and she felt she might faint—for real.

Elise DeFarge handed the microphone back to Loretta. "Last but definitely not least," Loretta trilled, "the man whose singular vision has so enhanced our concept of beauty—Philippe Noireau!" People sprang to their feet, applauding wildly, as a slim, silver-haired man in an elegant gray silk tuxedo appeared onstage.

"From so many beautiful girls," he said, his accent thicker than Elise's, "it was a terrible yet wonderful task to choose one who embodies Miss Noireau. There are three nominees—I will ask them to stand, please."

Michelle shrieked nervously. Through a fog of nausea, Kelly felt her heart leap expectantly. Paisley's whispered "Good luck!" came out hoarse and rough. Kelly closed her eyes, crossing her fingers in her lap, feeling a thrill of anticipation but already dreading the next moment—when her name would be announced and Chad would know the truth.

"Here goes nothing," Chad whispered, squeezing her hand proudly. Michelle was biting her lips, glaring at Kelly jealously. "Let the best girl win," she muttered. Kelly half-rose from her chair.

Philippe Noireau's voice echoed strong and clear in the room. "The nominees are—Jasmine, Augusta Morton, and Paisley Gregg."

"Paisley Gregg!" Michelle screamed. "I don't believe it!"

"Yahoo!" Chad leaped out of his chair, pulled Kelly upright, and hugged her. "I knew you could do it," he cried in her ear.

Gerard patted Paisley's hand sympathetically. "Don't worry, Sunny, you tried."

Two redheaded girls stood, and there was loud applause. Each girl's friends cheered loudly. Kelly froze inside Chad's embrace. "Congratulations, Sugar." Chad kissed her.

"Paisley Gregg," Kelly squeaked. "Uh—do they mean me Paisley or you Paisley?"

Paisley put a shaky hand to her throat. She looked stunned, and there were sudden tears in her eyes. "They mean m—me." Blindly, she groped at the table and stood up. "I made it, I'm a nominee!"

"You—you're not Paisley Gregg," Gerard said.

"Of course she is," Michelle said in disgust. "Look around—all redheads! I should have known!"

Kelly stared at the three girls standing up. "All redheads," she repeated in disbelief. Chad stared at Kelly.

"I did it; I got nominated," Paisley said over and over.

Dazed, Kelly pushed Chad away and dropped into her chair, hoping no one had noticed her standing. She'd never felt such complete humiliation. "I . . . I guess I'll sit down." Her hands and legs were shaking.

Chad grabbed her arm so hard it hurt. "What the *hell* is going on here?" he demanded. "I'm waiting, Sugar—or whatever your name is."

Kelly didn't answer him. "It was Paisley," she said weakly. "It wasn't me, it was Paisley. De-Farge was watching Paisley all along."

"And now," Philippe Noireau paused dramatically, "meet the new Miss Noireau . . ." A long drumroll sounded. Paisley reached out and grabbed Kelly's hand. "Wish me luck," she said desperately.

"Good luck!" Kelly whispered, choking. Michelle snorted.

"Miss Noireau—Augusta Morton!"

The room erupted into wild confusion as Augusta, a British model, leaped toward the stage, slim and vibrant in her pink satin Noireau gown. Her red hair glowing in a halo around her, she lifted a hand to Philippe Noireau. He kissed it and turned her toward the cameras.

There was total bedlam—flashbulbs popping, reporters shouting questions. Dimly, Kelly heard Chad talking to her, but she didn't even listen, she felt so sick. Michelle turned to hiss at her. "I could kill you, Kelly Blake. You tricked me! All week I copied you, thinking you were going to win. I should have known you were a loser!" Michelle stormed into the crowd.

"Here comes Meg," Paisley said weakly. Meg was indeed pushing her way toward their table. Shakily, Kelly rose to her feet.

Meg was grim. "I can't say I'm not sorry, girls. For you, and for me. But I'm also not surprised. Loretta told me DeFarge had her eye on Paisley all week. But you, Paisley, were so difficult to handle, so rude to Loretta, so untrustworthy, they didn't think it was worth the risk. Miss Noireau has to be responsible. She can't fake cramps or pull fainting spells during assignments."

Paisley's voice was a hoarse croak. "But I thought it was Kelly," she said, nearly strangling on the words. "I never thought I had a chance."

"You did." Meg was unyielding. "This season Noireau loves pale skin and red hair, like you and Jasmine and Augusta have. But he also loves a demure, quiet woman with an air of mystery. I'd say you blew that qualification."

Paisley sank onto her chair. The tears that had flooded her eyes spilled down her cheeks. "Me," she said dully, "it could have been me."

Meg turned to Kelly. "And you, Kelly, your behavior has been unforgivable. Since when do you miss curfew nearly every night? I thought you were more responsible than that. Both of you girls—I'll think twice before sending you or anyone under eighteen on an important over-night assignment again."

Kelly choked back her own tears. She'd been so sure she'd win—too sure, as it turned out. She should have left room for doubt.

"I never had a chance, did I?" she asked bitterly.

"No," Meg said simply. "You're much too theatrical for Noireau's taste. You just weren't the right type to begin with. That should be some comfort." She left them and went to congratulate Augusta and her agent.

Gerard pulled Paisley up by her elbow. "You deceived me, all this time. You lied to me—your name, your age—everything."

"Well, I did it for you," Paisley sobbed. "I had to, I was on probation—I had to use Kelly's name to get out at night."

"You made a fool of me," Gerard declared hotly, "in front of everyone I know. I thought our last night together would be a beautiful memory. Instead it's a—a nightmare of humiliation. I'm mortified, do you hear—mortified!"

Paisley abruptly stopped crying. She turned on

Gerard sharply. "Our last night . . . a memory? You mean we weren't going to see each other after tonight?"

"How could we do that, with you going back to New York tomorrow mornin'? But I thought we'd have ourselves a sweet farewell. Well, you can just forget that now."

"And you can forget me," Paisley shot back, her eyes sparkling with anger. "You and your sweet farewells! I could have won the title if it wasn't for you, you—you big tub of Texas lard!"

Gerard clapped his ten-gallon hat firmly on his head. "Sunny, you just lost yourself a place in my personal hall of fame."

"You—you—ooh!" Paisley snatched off the corsage Gerard had given her and hurled it at his head.

He caught it easily before it hit his hat. "Whooey," he said, grinning. "You're a real spitfire, honey, I'll say that."

"Get out," Paisley shrieked. "Get away from me, you—you hypocrite!" She stormed past Gerard, pushing her way out of the room.

Kelly looked up to find Chad gazing at her sadly. She could barely get the words out. "I'm so sorry, Chad, for everything. I can't explain."

To her surprise, he reached for her and drew her close. "It doesn't make any difference. Whatever your name is, I love you. You're still everything I want and need."

"But I'm not," Kelly blurted. "You don't even know my name. I'm not your sweet Sugar, I'm Kelly Blake. And there's a lot more to me than you think, Chad. I have ambitions, and plans . . ."

"I have plans, too, for you and me together. I need you, Sugar—Kelly. I need you to stay with me . . . to fill the empty places in my life."

"I can't," Kelly exclaimed. "Chad, when you called me Sugar, I felt like someone else—like the girl you wanted. But I'm not. I'm a phony, a hypocrite."

"Sugar, Kelly—nothing's impossible if you want it badly enough," Chad said stubbornly. "We'll have vacations and summers together, and when you turn eighteen we can be together for real. I'm . . . I'm asking you to marry me, Sugar."

Kelly felt a knifelike pain. "Oh, Chad," she cried, "don't, please. I—I've never felt so awful. Chad, you're lonely. You want someone, but I—I can't marry you. I can't even think about marriage. It would be like doors shutting me in, doors closing all around me. And doors should be opening for me, Chad. I'm looking forward to so many things! To being grown-up and on my own . . ."

Chad seemed not to be listening. "I know it will work out. No one could be more perfect for me."

"I'm not perfect for you! You want someone, anyone, so badly that you think it's me. But it isn't me, Chad. I know."

Finally Chad seemed to hear her. He pressed a fist to his forehead. "But I thought you loved me."

"I know." Kelly twisted her hands in anguish. "I thought I did. I guess it was a fantasy. A fantasy of finding the perfect boy, the perfect life."

"I could change," Chad cried.

Kelly shook her head, closing her eyes. "No, Chad. It's not you, it's me. You are perfect, for someone—but not me. Not me."

"I don't believe you," Chad said. "You wanted me, no more, no less."

"No, you're wrong," Kelly said, suddenly clear about everything. "I do want more—for both of us. You deserve more, someone who really is Sugar. And I need, well—someone who accepts the real me. I'm sorry, Chad. I didn't mean to hurt you."

They gazed at each other wordlessly. Kelly thought of the Triple C in all its rugged beauty. Then she shook her head and the vision disappeared. She had to make him understand what she only dimly understood herself. "I did love you, Chad, but not in the right way. I'm not even sure what the right way is, I just know it's something I haven't found yet. Saying yes to you would be . . . would be like saying no to myself." She spread her hands out helplessly. "Do you understand?"

Chad's face set in a stubborn expression. "There's someone else, isn't there? Someone back home."

"No, that's not it at all," Kelly insisted. "I haven't found anyone who's . . . completely right for me yet."

"I should have known you'd want an eastern boy after all."

"Oh, Chad, don't be like this." But she recognized his silence. He was closing her out, she realized, refusing to let her be different from what he wanted.

It was really over. She laid her hand on his arm gently. "Hey, I need—I need some sympathy myself tonight. This evening hasn't been easy for me."

Chad took his arm out from under her hand. "He's a lucky guy, whoever he is, your fellow back home." He spoke coldly. "I wish you both the best of luck."

"There isn't another guy," she protested, but Chad was already striding away from her. She watched him go, a jumble of emotions tormenting her. How could something be so *almost* right, so *almost* perfect? Despite everything, she would need a long time to let her memory of him go.

Around her, the crowd was heady with the excitement of the ball. Sadly, Kelly picked up her evening purse. She took one final glance around, then slowly pushed her way through the crowd.

The lobby was deserted, all the phone booths empty. Kelly took a deep breath, picked up a phone, dialed a number, and asked the operator who cut in to reverse the charges. On the second ring, Eric answered.

"Will you accept a collect call to Eric from Kelly?" the operator asked.

"I'll accept," Eric said promptly. "Kelly?"

She paused, uncertain. "Hi, Eric. It was probably dumb to call. I'll be back tomorrow."

He laughed. "Of course you should have called.

Hey, listen—I have some good news. Remember those hockey tickets I had?"

"Remember? We had a huge fight over them!"

"Not a huge fight," Eric said pleasantly, "you were just nervous about leaving the next day. I knew that."

"It was more than that, Eric." She tried to put all her feelings into words. "I guess I thought your plans came first with you, before my plans or feelings. What I'm trying to say is, I felt like you were taking me for granted." She shut her eyes; that was exactly how she'd felt about Eric, and that was why Chad had seemed so special— she'd come first with Chad, and she'd known it.

Eric's voice was hesitant. "I knew that was how you felt, Kelly. And I didn't know what to do about it, so I got mad at you. I don't know why. After you were gone, I felt pretty stupid about it, so I tried to pretend it never happened."

"Just tell me you missed me," Kelly said.

"I did. I really missed you." Kelly heard him clear his throat, and he sounded more normal, almost cheerful, when he spoke again. "So, anyway, I changed the stupid tickets. We can go to your skating party, all right?"

"Sure, I mean, that's great."

"Kelly, I really am glad you called. I did miss you. About that night—after you left Campy's, I went to get the tickets straightened out, and it took so long it was too late to call and say good-bye. I meant to come over the next morning, but I overslept and you were gone by the time I got there. And then Jennifer said you'd probably know I wasn't really mad at you, so I left it that way. I . . . I guess I should have called you in Houston and told you. I'm sorry."

What if he had? What if he'd called while she was with Chad—would she have forgiven Eric and told Chad good-bye? Feeling a little bit guilty, she said, "Oh, you didn't have to call, Eric. It was partly my fault; I was nervous and I did blow up at you. Besides, I—I've been awfully busy here."

"Yeah? So how was Houston, anyway?"

Suddenly she began to laugh. "Crazy," she said. "Really crazy. But I learned something, Eric. I learned how great it is to talk to someone like you—someone who really knows who I am." She paused, hesitating. "That sounds stupid. Do you understand what I'm trying to say?"

"I guess so," Eric said. "Maybe you can explain it to me at the skating party tomorrow night."

"Mmm . . ." Kelly said, laughing. "But maybe we can just concentrate on having a good time."

ABOUT THE AUTHOR

YVONNE GREENE was born in the Netherlands and emigrated to the United States as a young girl. At seventeen, she began a successful international modeling career, which she still pursues today. She has been featured on the pages of all the major American and European fashion magazines. Ms. Greene is also the author of two best-selling Sweet Dreams novels, *Little Sister* and *Cover Girl*, and *The Sweet Dreams Model's Handbook*.

Kelly Blake
TEEN MODEL

If you enjoyed reading this book, there are many other series published by Bantam Books which you'll love – SWEET DREAMS, SWEET VALLEY HIGH, CAITLIN, WINNERS, COUPLES and SENIORS. With more on the way – SWEPT AWAY and SWEET VALLEY TWINS – how can you resist!

These books are all available at your local bookshop or newsagent, though should you find any difficulty in obtaining the books you would like, you can order direct from the publisher, at the address below. Also, if you would like to know more about the series, or would simply like to tell us what you think of the series, write to:

Kim Prior,
Kelly Blake,
Transworld Publishers Ltd.,
61–63 Uxbridge Road,
Ealing,
London W5 5SA.

To order books, please list the title(s) you would like, and send together with a cheque or postal order made payable to TRANSWORLD PUBLISHERS LTD. Please allow the cost of the book(s) plus postage and packing charges as follows:

All orders up to a total of £5.00   50p
All orders in excess of £5.00   Free

Please note that payment must be made in pounds sterling; other currencies are unacceptable.

(The above applies to readers in the UK and Republic of Ireland only)

If you live in Australia or New Zealand, and would like more information about the series, please write to:

Sally Porter,
Kelly Blake,
Transworld Publishers (Aust) Pty Ltd.,
15–23 Helles Avenue,
Moorebank,
N.S.W. 2170,
AUSTRALIA

Kiri Martin,
Kelly Blake,
c/o Corgi and Bantam Books New Zealand,
Cnr. Moselle and Waipareira Avenues,
Henderson,
Auckland,
NEW ZEALAND